NOWHERE TO HIDE

Sigmund
Brouwer

Cover by Left Coast Design, Portland, Oregon

Cover photo © PlusONE / Shutterstock

NOWHERE TO HIDE

Published by Harvest House Publishers
Eugene, Oregon 97402
www.harvesthousepublishers.com

Library of Congress Cataloging-in-Publication Data
Brouwer, Sigmund
Nowhere to hide / Sigmund Brouwer.
pages cm
Sequel to: Dead man's switch.
Summary: High school senior computer experts William King and Blake Watt are picked up by the authorities to help them track down a father who has failed to make child-support payments, but as they learn more about the man they are searching for, they discover the true nature of their mission and learn the scary reason why they were chosen.

ISBN 978-0-7369-1748-3 (pbk.)
ISBN 978-0-7369-6306-0 (eBook)

[1. Computers—Fiction.] I. Title.
PZ7.B79984No 2015
[Fic]—dc23

2014034676

Printed in the United States of America

15 16 17 18 19 20 21 22 23 / BP-CD / 10 9 8 7 6 5 4 3 2 1

CHAPTER 1

On the morning that William Lyon Mackenzie King was betrayed by his father, drizzle blanketed the island, softening the light that filtered through the windows of his mother's workshop. She sat at a potter's wheel, working clay, molding it with wet hands, humming to herself as if King weren't sitting across from her on a cane-backed chair, leaning forward on his knees.

King felt as if the drizzle pressed a sanctuary upon them. Here on McNeil Island, it was quiet. Across the cold, deep waters of the southern end of Puget Sound, the Tacoma urban sprawl clawed its way north to connect with Seattle—a fabric of asphalt weaving frenzied lives, clusters of houses and apartments, and the endless signs of commercial properties competing for attention. There were no scheduled ferries from McNeil Island, no towns there, and only a few roads connecting the forty or so families who lived in identical houses overlooking identical gardens.

Yet McNeil Island was not the perfect sanctuary.

The houses were provided to employees of the prison on the island, which held some of the most violent men in the federal system. King wished he could believe the prison would always remain secure, protected as it was by massive walls, electronic surveillance, and thermal scanners.

He knew better. His mother, Ella, had nearly died because of the prison and the violent people in it. Since then, King could no longer walk carefree among the woods and pastures that had once seemed so idyllic. Only in Ella's workshop at the back of the house—where he could watch her at the wheel and listen to her hum in contentment—was King truly soothed of anxiety.

On this morning, the drizzle provided an extra layer of comfort. It shielded King from thoughts of the prison inmates and the imperfect men who guarded them. It buffered him from the world across Puget Sound, where Ella had spent weeks in a hospital in a coma. Here, King could see that his mother was safe, and he could cherish the illusion that the world outside did not exist.

The muted sound of cuckoo clocks from the house reached them, and Ella stopped humming, cocked her head, and smiled. King smiled with her. The cuckoo clocks were her idiosyncrasy. During the long weeks while she was across Puget Sound and alone in a coma, King and his father had let the cuckoo clocks wind down. During her absence, the cheerful sounds had been unbearable reminders of their shared loss.

"Cuckoo clocks," Ella said to King. She pushed back wisps of blonde hair that had fallen across her forehead. "That's something you won't hear at college. I'm going to miss you a lot. But you know that, right? I tell you that every day."

King had been homeschooled, a necessity because of the small population of the island. He'd been working hard to finish high school a year early. Everyone on the island knew of his vow to escape the island and chase big dreams.

"I've been thinking," King said. "You're able to do what you want from here on the island. Maybe that wouldn't be such a bad thing for me."

Ella made pottery, decorated and glazed it, and then offered it for sale online. She shipped her orders once a week and collected her money through PayPal. The Internet, as she said, put the whole world at her fingertips, and customers from Hong Kong to Amsterdam had proven her right.

"King," she laughed, "you'd go crazy if you stayed here."

He was beginning to believe the opposite was true, but he didn't dare tell her.

"You're too much like your dad," she said. "Mack was a wild one—needed to ramble and roam for a while."

That was part of the family legend, how Mack had been tamed by falling instantly in love with her.

All his life, King had loved thinking he would grow into the same strength and stubbornness that Mack possessed. Lately, however, that had felt like a burden. He needed to be himself, and if that meant delaying for a while the dreams of going out and tackling the world...

Those thoughts brought a physical reaction that King was learning to dread. His heart rate started climbing, and his lungs emptied of air. He drew in shallow gasps, hoping his mother wouldn't notice.

That's when Mack knocked on the door and walked in without waiting for an answer. Broad face. Broad shoulders. Mackenzie William King—Mack to everyone, including King, who'd been calling his dad Mack ever since King could swing a small baseball bat at the lobs Mack had loved tossing in the backyard.

Mack usually had a broad grin too. But not this morning.

King would realize later that the small twist of expression on Mack's face was a result of a father about to betray a son. But that realization would come too late for King to avoid the consequences.

"King," Mack said. "There's a helicopter on the way. Evans says your friends need you in the city."

A helicopter.

The skin at the base of King's throat began to tingle and then burn. He knew it was yet another symptom he would have to hide because both of his parents were watching to see how he would react to the news.

CHAPTER 2

King willed his exterior into stillness. Inside, however, his heart began to rev in an all-too-familiar pattern. A numbness began to run up the inside of each of his legs, and his abdomen began to tighten so hard he felt as if it would cramp.

"Helicopter," King repeated. He leaned back against his chair and faked a casual pose. That took effort because he remembered the last time he'd been in a helicopter—with a CIA guy named Evans—and the reason for it. Before his mother came out of her coma. An invisible hand seemed to tighten the grip around his throat.

"Rats," King said. "Just when this pottery was getting interesting, Evans decides to drop by."

The last few words came out in a gasp.

"You okay?" Ella asked.

King coughed and made a joke of it. "Hair ball."

Ella turned to Mack. "Are Blake and MJ in trouble?" Considering the way all of them had met Evans, it was a logical question.

"This probably isn't anything to panic about," Mack said to Ella.

King doubted his father realized the irony of those words. King had googled the symptoms he was fighting, so he knew he was on the verge of a full-blown panic attack.

"All Evans said was that Blake and MJ needed you," Mack continued, showing no awareness of what was hitting King. "For all I know, they're planning a surprise birthday party for you at a bowling alley."

Blake and MJ were King's friends. Since it was summer and school was out—even homeschoolers took a break—Blake and MJ had been off the island for a few days.

Evans was Central Intelligence Agency. More specifically, Evans was from the Special Operations Group division of the CIA. How weird that his family thought it was perfectly normal for someone from SOG to be on his way across Puget Sound by helicopter from Joint Base Lewis-McChord US military installation, just south of Tacoma. JBLM was a training institute and mobilization center. Evans served there as an instructor because SOG drew from the elite of the elite of the military divisions, including the Delta Force and SEAL teams.

"Great," King said, not meaning it. This small workshop was the perfect place to spend a contented, misty morning. He struggled to hide his efforts to pull air into his lungs.

"Thought you might like that," Mack said. "It seems like weeks since you've left the island. You must be going stir-crazy. And a helicopter, not a ferry. How cool is that?"

Actually, twenty-seven straight days on the island. King kept track. He'd been hoping to make it another twenty-seven days. Or another sixty days. Or more. He'd been trying to work up the courage to tell his parents he wasn't that interested in finishing high school early anymore. And to tell them he wasn't interested in college anymore either.

"Maybe..." King began, but the heavy throb-throb-throb of a helicopter interrupted him. *Maybe we can give Evans a quick call and tell him...*

And tell him what? King was running out of excuses to stay home. He'd managed to avoid going off the island with Blake and MJ a few days ago by pleading a stomach virus that was giving him the runs. With something like that, people didn't look for actual proof. They let you go to the bathroom, where you could flush the toilet every few minutes, spray a heavy dose of air freshener, and come out gagging at the smell as if you'd actually contributed something to the sewage system.

"What does King need to pack?" Ella asked. She obviously trusted that if Evans was behind it, all was good.

"Only his phone and wallet," Mack answered. "Evans said it was just a day trip."

The sound of the incoming helicopter grew thunderous. King could hardly believe he had once thought that would be the coolest thing in the world—having a Special Operations agent of the Central Intelligence Agency land a helicopter right in front of his house, right in the middle of his boring life on this obscure island. But that was before his friend Blake had set up something called a dead man's switch, before the coma that had almost taken away Ella, and before a chase that had almost killed Mack.

King now understood the ancient Chinese curse—"May you get what you wish for." Before the Dead Man's Switch episode, King had scorned the quiet island life and ached for adventure.

But then he'd gotten what he wished for. In triplicate. So on this morning, with a helicopter landing in front of his house, all he wanted was to lock himself in a closet and listen to himself breathe in the dark. The island was safe. Being off the island was not.

Maybe Mack was right. Maybe Blake and MJ were just planning a birthday party. If he was lucky, the rest of the day would include nothing more than a few games of bowling, and the hardest thing he'd have to do would be to act happy at a birthday party.

But really, would a CIA agent fly over in a helicopter for King just for that?

CHAPTER 3

Things started getting weird for King—weirder than a chopper with a CIA agent arriving to pick him up—when his best friend's mother unexpectedly appeared at the front door. She knocked once and opened it without waiting for an answer.

Actually, that wasn't the weird part. Mrs. Johnson did that all the time.

She stood there with a big smile and a small, taped cardboard box. The weird part was the conversation that followed.

She was a small woman, and when she walked, King thought of a crane tiptoeing through water, trying not to scare the minnows away.

"Hello, Mrs. Johnson," King said as he answered the door. He'd just put on his shoes and was about to head out to the helicopter. His parents were already outside on the front porch.

"I'd like you to take this to Michael," Mrs. Johnson said, extending the box.

The only families on the island were families with a prison employee. And the island was isolated because of the prison, so for as long as King could remember, his choice of friends was limited—especially new friends.

Blake Watt had arrived barely six months earlier. Until then, Michael Johnson had been the only boy on the island who was King's age. King's choice was simple—he could be friends with Johnson, or he could not have a friend.

As a result, the families got together for a shared meal at least once a week, and that meant that MJ's mother, Shirley, was almost a second mother to King.

Almost. King loved Ella and felt comfortable around her, but Mrs. Johnson was a control freak, a mother hen, and King never felt relaxed in her presence. King's mother made sure King did his homework and always assured him she didn't care if his grades were bad as long as he did his best and learned from his mistakes. Mrs. Johnson, on the other hand, always supervised MJ's homework, and when she found a mistake, she made sure MJ corrected it so he had perfect grades.

"No problem, Mrs. Johnson," King said as he accepted the box. "Happy to help."

It weighted little, so it obviously did not hold forty-eight cans of kidney beans as identified by large red letters across the side of it. No doubt Mrs. Johnson had taken it from the storage shed behind the Johnson house. The Johnsons did their shopping in bulk from Costco. Mrs. Johnson had been on a dietary kick the past few months, insisting that her husband and MJ get protein from vegetable sources instead of meat.

That had not been good for King. It meant that MJ wandered over as often as possible to look through King's fridge for leftover hamburgers or steak. Bad enough that it was taking food from King's mouth, but MJ and beans were a bad combination. MJ never apologized—not for taking leftovers as if they belonged to him, and not for his digestive system's efforts to deal with the beans. MJ's cholesterol level might have been dropping, but his gas level had risen dramatically.

King waited for detailed instructions from Mrs. Johnson on exactly when and how to give the box to MJ, as if King were a three-year-old.

"Is your stuff for the hotel already in the helicopter?" Mrs. Johnson asked.

"Well…"

"MJ didn't let me do his packing for him," she said. "I don't know why in the world he'd stop me."

Because he wants to be a grown-up, King thought. But this wasn't the time for that conversation. There would never be a good time for that conversation.

"Who knows if he has enough underwear?" Mrs. Johnson continued. "And socks. A person needs lots of underwear and socks, so that's what's in the box. Cleaned with a detergent that doesn't make Michael itch. He's so sensitive, you know. When that rash goes down the inside of his legs—"

"I'll make sure to give him the box," King said. He did not, as in not ever, want to hear about any kind of rash that involved MJ. Mrs. Johnson liked to be explicit when it came to medical problems.

"You packed enough underwear, right?" she asked.

"Yes," King said. It wasn't a lie. He supposed if it came down to it, he would wash what he was wearing with dish detergent in a sink and dry it with a hair dryer, and it would be ready to wear in five minutes or less. Besides, hadn't Evans said all that King needed was his phone and wallet?

"I'm sure they are going to split the reward with you," Mrs. Johnson said. "Even if you arrive after they've done all the work."

Her voice carried faint disapproval of King, but he'd learned not to pay attention to it. Instead, his mind naturally turned to two questions.

Reward? Work?

"I'm going to run now," Mrs. Johnson said. "No time for chitchat. Sorry."

She paused and looked at King. "You won't lose that box, right? And you'll give it to MJ right away, right?"

"Yes, Mrs. Johnson," King said. "I'd hate for MJ to get a rash."

CHAPTER 4

King had no difficulty remembering the first time he had been in a helicopter. And, no coincidence, it was when he first met Evans. His second time in a helicopter had been with Evans too. This would be his third.

The first helicopter had been a small civilian unit, like the ones used to monitor traffic, piloted by Evans. The second helicopter had been a UH-1 gunship—Evans called it a Huey—that bristled with missiles and was big enough to hold the commando unit that accompanied them.

Naturally, King expected Evans would be in the small commuter chopper that had just landed on the road in front of his house. No one worried about traffic safety on McNeil Island. Except for a few vehicles used for official prison purposes, nobody owned cars. People walked or rode bicycles.

But King was proven wrong. He stood beside Mack and Ella at their front porch and saw that the pilot who stepped out of the chopper was not Evans. The man was Caucasian, not African-American like Evans. The only similarity was that this man wore a well-tailored suit, just as Evans did. This man's suit was charcoal gray; King remembered that Evans preferred navy blue.

"Don Mundie," the man barked as he stepped beyond the slowing helicopter blades and held out a badge for identification.

Mundie was tall and thin with neatly cut blond hair. He wore Oakley sunglasses—black lenses—and his face had the kind of wrinkles that came from facing sun and wind. He was probably past his mid-forties and could have been older. He walked like an athlete, like a man who was accustomed to winning tournaments at his golf club.

Hurrying beneath the roof of the front porch to keep his suit from getting soaked in the drizzle, Mundie continued holding out the badge until he was close enough for Mack to examine it.

Mack grunted approval, and Mundie slipped the badge inside his suit jacket.

"And I know who you are," Mundie said. "Evans sent me photos. Nice to meet you. Mack and Ella and William."

Not William. But King. William Mackenzie King, a reversal of the first two names of his father. Ella's mother, a Canadian, had slipped in a second middle name so that King's full name was William Lyon Mackenzie King. It had been a long time before anyone realized why—that was the name of a former Canadian prime minister.

"Nice to meet you," Mack said, allowing Ella to shake Mundie's hand first and then doing the same. Nobody corrected Mundie for addressing King as William. But to King, it was a tiny red flag. Evans never called King by that name.

"Nice to meet you," King said, accepting Mundie's offered handshake. Even though it wasn't nice to meet anyone. King wanted to go back to the workshop and let the drizzle protect him from the world.

"Coffee?" Mack asked Mundie. "Cup of tea?"

Mundie shook his head no.

"We were expecting Evans," Ella said. "He made it sound like it was something personal on short notice. King and Evans have a history. A good history."

"I'm aware of both," Mundie said. "That you might be expecting

Evans, and that this isn't really official. As you know, Evans wants to keep all of this under the radar."

All of what, King wondered. What was supposed to be under the radar? He thought Mack might ask the same thing.

"And you will have it wrapped up by evening?" Mack said.

To King, that implied Mack knew what was going on. Worse, it implied Mack knew what was going on *and* was keeping it from King. It was a mild betrayal but still a betrayal of sorts. Unless this really was a surprise birthday, Mack should have been open with King. Especially after all that they had been through with Evans when Ella was in her coma. But this wasn't a surprise party, King was certain. Not with a helicopter involved.

"Probably have it wrapped up earlier than evening," Mundie said. "With luck, Evans can fly King back. He got tied up with something at the last minute. That's all I can say. It's a matter of national security."

Mundie grinned as Ella's eyes widened in alarm.

"Standard agency joke," Mundie said, leaving his grin in place. "With the CIA, everything is national security. Even something as boring as stopping for a cup of coffee."

King found a way to put a grin on his own face. "Two creams, two sugars. Evans didn't like anything else but that. Got fussy when I didn't put enough sugar in it."

"That's Evans," Mundie said. "When we're in the air, he'll probably call and tell me to make a Starbucks run."

"Not Tim Horton's?" King asked.

"Tim Horton's?" Mundie said.

"Standard family joke," King said. "Tim Horton's is a Canadian franchise. My mother is Canadian. Everybody there loves Tim Horton's."

"Hah," Mundie said. "Your family joke isn't much funnier than our CIA joke."

"Hah," King said, feeling the panic symptoms surge back again.

As Mundie began to lead him to the helicopter, it took every ounce of determination for King to move one foot in front of the other and follow. Not only was King feeling the dread that came with thoughts of leaving the island, but now he knew something was wrong with this scenario.

Evans always took his coffee black. So why had this guy, Mundie, just lied?

CHAPTER 5

The drizzle became light rain as the helicopter lifted and headed east from McNeil Island. With visibility reduced, the prison buildings at the corner of the island were blurred to King as Mundie maneuvered over the shoreline and continued toward Tacoma. Or maybe the blurring was a problem with his eyes.

He'd done his homework on panic attacks. Who wanted to admit to anyone he was going crazy? King wanted to keep it to himself.

First, a few possible other causes: phobias, chronic illness, hyperventilation syndrome, short-term triggering causes, or biological causes.

Well, his self-diagnosis ruled out phobias. He didn't have any.

He was healthy, so it wasn't a chronic illness then.

Hyperventilation? That meant overbreathing, resulting in too much oxygen and not enough carbon dioxide in the bloodstream. But his panic attacks didn't follow any overbreathing. Instead, they led to overbreathing. So no, it wasn't hyperventilation.

Short-term triggering causes included significant personal loss or significant life changes. Nope. He'd *nearly* lost his mother to the coma, but he had not lost her, and until the coma he'd been looking forward to a significant life change—leaving the island for the freedom of the outer world.

So King was down to suspecting a biological cause for the attacks. He didn't have symptoms for suspected underlying conditions like hypoglycemia or hyperthyroidism or Wilson's disease or pheochromocytoma or labyrinthitis. Googling each of those conditions just to learn what they were and eliminate them as possibilities had taken him hours.

There was, however, one possible biological cause that had jumped out at him. Post-traumatic stress disorder. Something that sometimes happened to soldiers and firemen and policemen either after long-term and continued stress or after a particularly high-stress situation—like the dead man's switch episode King had survived a month earlier, which was the reason his mom nearly died in a coma.

Yeah. King would say he qualified as a survivor of a high-stress situation.

Some people with PTSD got depressed and angry and lost their appetite. Others were suddenly and without warning inflicted by panic attacks.

For King, that included a choking impulse, unexpected trembling, tingling sensations, sweating, and feeling as if the world was going dark and he was looking through a tunnel.

Like now. Strapped into a helicopter, leaving the sanctuary of a quiet room, where he knew he was safe and his mother was safe with him.

He'd wanted to bolt before entering the helicopter, wanted to run back to his bedroom in the house and crawl into bed and pull the blanket over his head and sob.

But that would have been abandoning his friends. Something was wrong about this situation.

As Mundie flew the helicopter toward the city across Puget Sound, King was terrified by the sensations. The shaking of the chopper, the occasional short drops through air pockets, the noise. The only thing that drove him forward and kept him from giving in to the panic was an even bigger and even more stabbing fear.

If he didn't do this—with a degree of intelligence unclouded by his growing panic—he was worried that bad things could possibly happen to his friends.

King clung to the straps over his shoulders and told himself to think, think, think. Not feel, feel, feel.

What was going on? How could he prepare himself to manage the situation—whatever it might be—in the best way possible?

CHAPTER 6

A person could assume that if a hotel had a heliport on the roof, it was the type of hotel where guests dropped an American Express card on the counter and expected to spend for a night what most people spent for a week in other hotels.

King's assumption was confirmed when a uniformed bellhop waited for the helicopter blades to stop rotating and then dashed through the rain with an umbrella. He held it over Mundie and King as they walked across the rooftop toward an elevator door.

It wasn't Tacoma, but Seattle. Downtown Seattle.

The hotel was surrounded by other buildings of similar height, and Mundie had shown his expertise by clearing the flight pattern, alerting the hotel manager of his impending arrival, and setting the helicopter down with hardly a bump.

The rooftop wasn't the place to bolt for escape from Mundie. Nor would that be intelligent. If King bolted, that would alert Mundie to King's suspicions. And if King's friends really were in danger, that would only make things worse.

Maybe, King wanted to believe, they weren't in danger at all. Maybe his paranoia was another symptom of the panic attacks. But he couldn't find a way to convince himself otherwise—Evans drank his coffee black, not with two creams and two sugars.

Maybe Mundie's lie was a tiny lie, so maybe it didn't mean anything. Maybe this was an irrational fear because of King's panic attacks. But why would Evans send Mundie to get King, without Mundie knowing that Evans never called King by his first name of William?

Inside the elevator, the bellhop—short and wide with hair curling out from beneath his red cap—pressed the button for the lobby floor.

Mundie reached over and pushed the button for the tenth floor.

"Already checked in," Mundie said. "We're all good."

"Yes, sir," the bellhop said.

No further conversation.

The elevator slowed in total silence. The doors opened, and King followed Mundie into the hallway. The carpet was expensive, and large, framed prints hung on the walls.

"You've been quiet," Mundie said. "No questions about why your friends need you?"

"Evans sent you, right?" King replied. "My friends and parents and I trust him completely."

"He trusts you guys too," Mundie said. "I've read the reports on what we started calling the Dead Man's Switch episode at the agency. I can see why."

Then Mundie frowned. "You okay?"

King was shaking. He could feel the sweat on his face. He wanted to stop and lean on the wall and draw in huge gasps of air.

"Just getting over something," King said. "Same thing that kept me from coming here a few days ago. Nothing to worry about. It's not contagious."

Mundie nodded.

They stopped at room 1010.

Mundie knocked, and King heard approaching footsteps inside.

"Stand in front of the peephole," Mundie said. "They'll need to see you before they open the door."

Was this why Mundie had needed King? To get the door open? Was

King betraying his friends by going along with this? Or was the danger all in King's imagination? If it wasn't his imagination, was this the time to run? After all, if Mundie needed King to get inside the room, maybe running would be the best way to protect Blake and MJ.

Too late. MJ swung the door open.

"Kinger!" MJ said in his radio announcer voice that he thought was cool but no one else did. "Glad you made it. You feeling better?"

MJ—Michael Johnson—was tall, gangly, and working hard on a mustache. If MJ's hair had been blond, his mustache would have been invisible. Instead, because he had dark hair, the mustache looked like a smudge of dirt. And MJ was proud of it.

MJ gave Mundie a questioning glance.

"Evans sent me to pick up William and bring him to you guys," Mundie said, pushing his way inside.

William. A warning flag. Or not?

"I'm CIA," Mundie continued. "Need to see a badge?"

"Uh..." MJ said.

King could tell that MJ was still trying to figure out why Mundie had called King by his first name of William.

Without waiting for an answer, Mundie pushed past MJ down the short hallway. King stayed with Mundie. The hallway opened to a large suite that had a view of the Seattle waterfront. An open door led to a bedroom. There was a big, luxurious couch in the suite. It still had blankets and sheets and a pillow, as if either Blake or MJ slept in the bedroom and the other out in the suite. The sheets were folded neatly with the blanket, so King guessed it was Blake.

Empty pizza boxes were stacked on a counter that separated the open suite from a small kitchen area. Beside the boxes were empty soda cans, stacked neatly. That would have been Blake's work. Blake bordered on obsessive compulsive.

Blake Watt barely looked up from a couple of computer screens on a desk against the far wall. Directly between both screens was an iPad on a stand, its screen black.

"Hey, King," Blake said. "Good to see you."

The computers and monitors were obviously not part of the hotel suite. Cables snaked from the desk to outlets and to a printer on a smaller desk nearby.

Blake's chair was on wheels. He swung sideways a few feet to look at the other monitor and then did some rapid-fire keyboarding, still ignoring King and Mundie.

Blake was fourteen and looked eleven. Skinny and blond. He wore a Minecraft T-shirt. Anyone who looked closely would see small circular scars on his arms. King knew they were burn marks from cigarettes. That too had been part of the Dead Man's Switch events, all started by Blake and his computer expertise.

Mundie walked to the screen.

"Huh," Mundie said after a few moments of observation. "Drone surveillance."

That's when Blake seemed to realize someone else had entered the room with King and that the someone else hadn't been Evans.

Blake swung away from the screen.

"Who are you?" Blake said bluntly. "Why are you here?"

"Evans sent me," Mundie said. "He wants an update."

"Code phrase?" Blake asked.

"Code phrase," Mundie repeated.

"MJ," Blake said, his irritation making him sound ten years older. "You let someone in without a code phrase? Evans said—"

"He's got a badge," MJ said. "He came with King."

Blake stood and faced Mundie squarely. He was half Mundie's size.

"Sir," Blake said. "If you don't have the code phrase, you're going to have to leave the room."

"Good work," Mundie said. "Evans wanted me to test you. That's partly why I'm here."

Mundie was focused on Blake, and Blake was focused on Mundie. That gave King the chance to slide toward Mundie's back. King was so intent on what he needed to do, some of the symptoms of his panic seemed to slip away.

King undid his belt and pulled it free of his pants loops. He slid the belt back through the buckle and left it looped.

"Glad I passed the test," Blake said. "Now let's see you do the same."

As King held his belt in one hand and tiptoed a final step toward Mundie and Blake at the computers, he marveled at Blake's toughness. But then Blake was so tough he had not given answers to a man with a lit cigarette. That's why Blake had so many of those circular scars on his arms.

"Today's code phrase," Mundie said, "is that—"

King didn't let Mundie finish. He flipped the belt loop over Mundie's head and yanked the noose tight. He pulled hard, staggering Mundie backward.

"Pillowcase," King said to MJ as Mundie clawed at his own neck to relieve the pressure. "Shake it loose so you can put it over his head!"

To Blake, King said, "Your belt. Around his ankles."

King gave a violent tug on the end of his belt and toppled Mundie, rolling him onto his stomach. King jumped on the man's back, still pulling the belt as if it were a choke chain.

Mundie kicked as hard as he could but was helpless to roll onto his back.

"Hurry, MJ," King said. "Pillowcase."

King had learned that MJ was a klutz in all situations except when it really mattered, and then MJ had a steel that seemed impossible for a gangly kid who always tried so hard to act cool that he looked just the opposite.

MJ had the pillowcase over Mundie's head in seconds.

"Sit on his legs," Blake grunted to MJ. "He's kicking too hard."

With MJ's help, Blake managed to tighten his own belt around Mundie's ankles. Then they fought Mundie's arms and managed to tie them behind his back with shoelaces.

Only then did King relieve the pressure of his belt around Mundie's neck. He remembered when a real choke chain had been put around his neck and how close he'd come to dying.

"You guys are making a huge mistake," Mundie said. "And trust me, you and Evans are going to pay for this. I'm calling this operation over."

"I've got to go with him on the huge mistake part," MJ said to King. "You sure about all this?"

"Code phrase," Blake repeated. "If he gives us the code phrase, we'll let him go. No harm, right?"

Silence from beneath the pillowcase.

"Satisfied we did the right thing?" Blake asked MJ.

"But we just jumped a CIA agent," MJ said.

"Call Evans," King told MJ. "Ask him if he sent Mundie."

King began to feel the panic attack return. This time, however, he didn't hide his efforts to pull in lungfuls of air.

"Hold on," Blake said, looking past them at the computer screens. "Check out the drones on monitor one."

CHAPTER 7

King leaned over Mundie and spoke quietly. "Man, I'd hate to do this to you, because MJ only changes his socks twice a week, but if you start yelling, we're going to shove them in your mouth."

"Hey," MJ said. "I change them—"

King made a cutting motion across his throat. Not the time to mention that he'd brought a box with clean socks and underwear from Mrs. Johnson.

"Oh," MJ mouthed, suddenly realizing Mundie needed to think MJ had smelly socks.

"We're good?" King asked Mundie.

"Good," he said in a quiet voice. "But I'm calling in for help. This operation is over."

King thought it was weird for Mundie to repeat this, but events were flashing too quickly for him to give it more consideration.

"No phone for you then," MJ said to Mundie as King moved past MJ to look at monitor one. "Not that you'd be able to dial anyway."

MJ was the only person to laugh.

King took in the monitor view to see the roof of a mobile home with a rickety fence and an old truck parked on a driveway. Dark

SUVs were parked in front, and a dozen members of a SWAT team were moving into position around the perimeter of the mobile home.

"Got the drones on autopilot," Blake said. "Just circling at about 3000 feet. Nobody below has a clue we're up there. Military grade stuff. Very cool."

And very expensive, King thought. Very, very expensive. Where did Blake get this kind of money, and why was he in this hotel room?

Blake made a few keystrokes, and the camera zoomed in close enough on one of the SWAT soldiers to see the smoked-glass cover of his helmet.

"Obviously something is happening," Blake said. "MJ and I have been monitoring the place for a couple of days. No one went in or out. Now this. You show up, and the action starts."

"That's our man," MJ said. "The Kinger. Rocking and rolling. He always makes stuff happen."

On the screen, King saw the SWAT guy tilt his head as if scanning the sky. He pointed upward and made a motion for someone else to respond.

"Zoom back," King said to Blake. "See if anyone else is looking up at us."

"Wouldn't be at our drone," Blake said. "Its wingspan is only about six feet. As high as it is, it's invisible and silent. The military has controllers in Colorado, buzzing the skies of Afghanistan with drones like these. They lock in on a target, and bam, it's like a lightning bolt from out of nowhere."

"Humor me," King said. "The guy was looking up for a reason. It's like he's calling for a shot."

More clicking. King reached toward the screen and pointed without touching. He knew Blake hated having anyone touch the screen. He knew it because MJ always forgot and touched the screen and Blake always elbowed MJ in the gut.

"There," King said. "The guy with what looks like a bazooka."

Blake whistled. "Missile launcher."

"Where exactly is this?" King asked, thinking if it was in a city somewhere, firing a missile wasn't a great idea.

"High desert east of the Cascades," Blake said. "The guy lives in the middle of nothing. I'll zoom out and show you how sandy and dry it is."

"No need," King said. "You're not concerned about the guy with the missile launcher? That's who I'd be watching. He's pointing it right at the drone's camera."

"Probably going to fire a warning shot to scare the guy inside. To me, that's the bigger question—why are they taking this guy down? No way the shooter knows about the drone, and no way he could hit it at our altitude."

A flash came from the missile launcher. It was eerie to watch the action because it was in total silence.

"He's shooting at something," King said.

"Ten..." Mundie's voice reached them as he counted in slow cadence. "Nine...eight...seven..."

"Ignore him," Blake said.

"What's on the other monitor?" King asked. "Looks like the hotel hallway."

Four guys in suits were walking sideways, swiveling their heads to glance up and down the hallway for danger. They had their hands inside their suit jackets, as if ready to reach for pistols.

"Six...five...four..." Mundie continued from beneath the pillowcase over his head.

"Crap," Blake said. "Our hotel hallway."

"Three...two...one..." Mundie said. "The drone down yet?"

The first monitor went dark.

"Crap," Blake said again. "He hit our drone. Impossible."

"You guys have nowhere to hide," Mundie said. "Now we're about to rock and roll my way. My guys should be busting down the door in ten...nine...eight..."

CHAPTER 8

"Okay," MJ said in a high-pitched voice. "What we do is light the room on fire. It will set off a smoke detector and—"

"MJ!" King said. "We'll be *in* the burning room."

"Six..." Mundie said. "Five..."

King was irritated. Not scared. Not mad. He should have been scared and mad. But the countdown thing was getting old fast. He was so irritated he had no sense of panic. Not much could go worse at this point.

King leaned over and tugged his right shoe loose. He peeled off his sock and rolled it into a ball. He took the few steps toward Mundie's prone body, rolled the man on his back, and ripped the pillowcase loose.

Sure, they were about to get taken down by suit guys for something that King had no clue about, but King wasn't going to listen to Mundie anymore.

Mundie saw the sock and snapped his mouth shut.

King imagined he heard someone call Mundie's name. Then he realized he *had* heard it.

Mundie was wearing a nearly invisible earpiece. Which meant he was probably wired for sound going out too. That's why he'd said he was calling the operation over.

King visualized the room number on the door, from when he'd stood with Mundie, waiting for MJ to swing it open.

1010.

King leaned in, putting his mouth close to Mundie's face. King spoke in a low growl.

"Hurry, guys. Don't mess up. Room 1009."

"At the door," Blake said. "At the door!"

A high-pitched scream reached them from another room. The scream grew louder and more indignant.

"King," Blake whispered from the monitor. "They hit the wrong room!"

Mundie opened his mouth, and King was ready for it. He jammed his sock deep, and Mundie made a gagging sound.

"How's that taste?" MJ crowed.

King made another slicing sound across his throat to urgently cut off MJ and then bounced over to Blake and tapped Blake's shoulder, motioning for quiet.

On the monitor, the suit guys were back in the hallway, milling with confusion. A big woman in a nightgown followed them into the hallway and began beating on the suit guy nearest her.

King pointed at Mundie and whispered. "No noise. He's wired. I think he called them in after we tackled him."

King tiptoed back to Mundie and made sure the sock was in place.

Mundie's eyes were wide with rage. King gave it some thought and realized he probably had gone an extra day or two with the same pair of socks. Not fun to be Mundie right now.

King leaned over and pulled the earpiece loose and held it close to his own ear.

"Mundie, come in," a disembodied voice said. "Come in—we need direction here."

King's guess had been accurate. He had no idea why Mundie was doing all of this and why he needed four suit guys to back him up, but

King did have a sense of what the suit guys were up against. This was an expensive, upscale hotel. They couldn't go from door to door, kicking each one down. Who knew how many other large, indignant women were ready to attack?

"Mundie?" came a voice from the earpiece. "Mundie? You switched us to 1009. Wrong room. Back to 1010?"

King lifted Mundie's suit jacket open and saw the wire. It led to a small microphone clipped to the inside suit pocket.

King crouched and said in another low growl. "I've got you on monitor. Two rooms down. Other side. Move."

Mundie managed a quiet muffled grunt of rage behind the sock.

King smiled at him and gently patted Mundie's face. At this point, King felt no remorse at what he'd done to Mundie. Whatever was happening, Mundie had tried to set up a trap.

If he and Blake and MJ could get out of the hotel, maybe his two friends could help King understand what was happening.

"They're using a room key again," Blake whispered from his surveillance position at the monitor. "Someone must have given them a master to all the doors."

And another loud scream. Then howling of outrage.

"Mundie!" the voice yelped into the earpiece. "What are you doing to us?"

King went back to the monitor. Sure enough, the guys in suits were back in the hallway. The first big woman hadn't left them alone, and a second woman, equally large, was out in the hallway too. She was armed with an umbrella. After all, this was Seattle.

The monitor showed the guys in the suits fleeing to the fire escape at the end of the hallway. The two women gave each other high fives, and once they were sure the hallway was clear, each ducked back to her own room.

King knelt back down beside Mundie and yanked loose the mike. He twisted the wire and snapped it, careful to make sure nothing happened to the earpiece.

"Mundie?" a voice said into the earpiece. "Mundie? Mundie?"

"Looks like we have a little time for a chat," King said to Mundie.

"You can't talk to them, but I'll be happy to listen to what you have to say. Want the sock out?"

Mundie nodded.

King pulled it.

Mundie drew some air in. King saw it coming. The man was going to shout. King popped the sock in again, thinking maybe it had been three days with the same pair of socks, not two.

King stood.

"Well, gentlemen," he said to Blake and MJ. "He's not going to talk. Maybe you two can tell me what's going on. But not here. We have to get away from this room."

"Maybe," Blake said, pointing at the hallway monitor. "Maybe not."

King went back to the monitor and looked for himself. A man was walking down the hallway, straight for room 1010.

Evans.

CHAPTER 9

MJ ran to the short hallway of the suite and opened the door for Evans.

King stood right behind MJ and held his finger over his lip to indicate silence.

"No thanks," King said for Mundie's benefit. "No maid service right now."

King elbowed MJ to keep MJ quiet. Then King put his finger on his lip to indicate silence again.

Evans nodded and stepped inside and shut the door.

King held up two hands, palm outward, instructing Evans to wait.

Evans nodded again.

King marched back into the suite and put the pillowcase back over Mundie's head. No point in letting Mundie know Evans had arrived.

King went back to the short hallway and waved Evans into the suite.

Evans joined the three of them at the monitors. He wore his customary navy-blue suit but had the build and balance of a man who was anything but a banker. He had cropped black hair without a tinge of gray despite the wrinkles forming at the corners of his eyes. The intensity of those nearly black eyes ensured they would never be lost against the deep-black skin of his face.

King didn't know if Evans was his first name or his last name. He and Blake and MJ didn't know much about Evans. He worked for the Special Operations Group in the CIA. He was based out of the Tacoma–Seattle area. He'd stepped in at a crucial time during Dead Man's Switch, choosing to back King over a high-ranking prison official. And his name was Evans. Only Evans.

Evans flicked his eye downward. He saw Mundie on the floor, the shoelaces that bound Mundie's hands, the belt that bound his feet, and the pillowcase over his face.

King handed Evans a pad of hotel stationery and a pen. It was obvious by now that silence was important.

Evans scrawled some words and pointed at Blake.

All good with data backed up?

Blake nodded.

Evans wrote again. *Scramble the hard drives. We don't have time to take them. But we'll take the iPad.*

Blake scooted to the keyboard.

Evans pointed at King, and made a turning motion with his right forefinger and thumb pressed together. Then Evans pointed at Mundie and made the same motion again.

Keys, King thought.

King held his hands out as if he were holding a steering wheel and motioned as if he were driving.

Evans shook his head and with one hand made a lasso circling motion.

Ah, King thought. *Helicopter. Who knew that helicopters had keys?*

King bent down beside Mundie and gingerly patted the man's front pockets. Mundie flinched. He was blind to the world and hadn't known the touch was coming.

King had a burst of inspiration.

"I'm sure I've already broken a dozen federal laws already," King said to Mundie. "So why not take what I can? Credit cards should come in handy. Government expense account, right?"

King patted more pockets, pulling everything out that he could.

Breath mints, two sets of keys. One with a Volvo logo, obviously for the vehicle Mundie had taken to the office to start the day. Another set that must be for the helicopter.

"Great," King said to Mundie. "I know where your office is. Looks like we'll have wheels. Might be a day or two before someone comes looking for you. Cash, credit card, and a fast car. We'll be a thousand miles away by the time you get out of that pillowcase."

Evans gave King a thumbs-up. Evans understood. They were taking the chopper, but King was trying to buy some time by fooling Mundie into believing otherwise, even if it only bought them an extra ten or fifteen minutes before Mundie called in a missing Volvo and then went to the roof. If they did get far enough away, King knew they'd have to make sure to call the front desk and send someone to the room to rescue Mundie. That way, the worst thing to happen to Mundie was that he'd wet his pants.

King tucked the stolen wallet in his pocket and handed the second set of keys to Evans, who nodded in satisfaction. Evans tapped King on the shoulder and made a "let's roll" signal, and King, Blake, and MJ followed Evans out of the hotel room.

Finally, King thought, he'd get answers.

A muffled *mmmppppph* from the pillowcase stopped them. Evans gave King the go-ahead to look.

King went back to Mundie and leaned over. "You won't yell if I pull the sock."

Mundie grunted something that sounded like uh-uh.

King reached underneath and yanked the sock.

Mundie let out a gasp as if a cork had been popped from a bottle. He spoke in a low voice from the pillowcase. "Here's one chance for you to make a deal. I know Evans is behind this. Let me go and then help me find Evans. There won't be any consequences for you three."

Evans glanced at King and then at Blake and then at MJ, knowing they'd have to make a decision.

"Whatever is happening here," Mundie said, "Evans is conning you. Untie me now, and we'll clear up the misunderstanding and get you back to your parents like this never happened."

King pointed at the door, a clear indication he was choosing Evans over Mundie. Blake and MJ gave emphatic nods.

"Boys?" Mundie said. "Boys? Answer me. Because if you don't untie me, every law-enforcement officer in the state is going to be looking for you within the hour."

King waited until the room was clear to pull the pillowcase up again. Mundie glared at him but saw the sock and said nothing.

So King pinched the man's nose, and when Mundie gasped for air, King shoved the sock in again. He left the pillowcase on the floor and ran to catch the others.

CHAPTER 10

In the hallway, unaware of what King had done, Evans said, "Mundie can yell all he wants now. We don't have far to go." He motioned for them to hurry with him to the far end.

"I put the sock back in his mouth," King said.

With Blake and MJ right behind him, King expected Evans to keep moving and bolt through the exit door that led to the stairs. Instead, Evans reached the hotel room beside the exit door and stopped. With a smooth motion, he pulled out a room key, opened the door, and pointed the three inside.

King was in first. The suite was identical to the one they'd left behind, but it was a lot neater.

Blake and MJ tumbled in behind him, and then Evans slid the door shut.

King was breathing hard, more from running than from panic. But the panic wasn't far beneath the surface.

"King," Evans said, extending his hand. "It's about time you joined the team. Good to see you."

"And you too," King said, accepting the handshake. He just wished it wasn't in a situation like this.

"All good with the stomach flu?" Evans said.

"Sir?"

"Mack said you had some kind of bug. Kept you in the bathroom a lot. Too bad. We could have used your help earlier."

King felt a stab of conscience. He'd flat-out lied about that. To his parents. And by extension, to his friends and to Evans. It occurred to him that the lie hurt King more than it did his friends.

"Speaking of all the time you were on the toilet," MJ said to King, "I left my box of clean underwear in the other room. Mom is going to kill me."

Despite himself—or maybe because he'd been so stressed and this was a good way to break his tension—King laughed. It felt like his first real laugh in a long time.

"Seriously?" King said to MJ. "You're more worried about your mom than the senior CIA agent we just assaulted?"

"Yeah." MJ was indignant. "I'm not an idiot."

Blake nodded. "I'm with MJ. You don't want his mom mad at you."

"Besides," MJ said, "Evans has us covered."

MJ looked at Evans. "Right?"

"Right," Evans said. He moved to an open suitcase on the floor and came up with a pair of socks and tossed them at King. "Just what you needed."

King smiled and pulled off his other sock so he could wear a matching pair. He laced up his shoes.

"You've got more for us than a pair of extra socks," MJ said to Evans.

"In about a half hour, we'll be on a helicopter and safely away from here," Evans said. "It's all good."

"Sure," King said. He felt his throat tighten. The action was over, and that gave him time to think about panic. "It's all good…as soon as you explain what's happening."

Evans said, "I've got a few rooms booked under different names and credit cards at this hotel. Just for an event like this. Mundie can't do a room-to-room search.

"See?" MJ said. "And we've got the keys to Mundie's helicopter."

"That's not what I meant," King said. "What's going on? Why do you have the other room and the monitor and a drone and a whole SWAT team taking down the guy in the mobile home?"

"Repeat that," Evans said, going very still.

"Just as Mundie and I got into the other room," King said, "a SWAT team captured a guy."

"No," Evans said softly. "Impossible. Mundie knew about that?"

Blake said, "We thought you'd ordered the SWAT team."

Evans didn't reply. He just sucked in air through his nostrils with a deep intake of frustration.

"But we have the getaway helicopter," MJ said. "Right?"

"Which we won't take," Evans said. "I'm sure one of Mundie's guys is up on the roof waiting for him—or for us. I just wanted the keys so he wouldn't be able to take it himself. Anything to slow him down is okay."

"And the other guys on his team..." King said, although he could guess. "They'll be at different locations in the hotel, watching the exits?"

Sooner or later, King needed to ask exactly why Mundie and his men were after Evans.

Evans shook his head to the negative. "More than likely they'll be in the office with all the monitors for the hotel surveillance system. He probably had one guy there the entire time."

Now it was King's turn to draw in a sharp breath. "Then he saw us running from room 1010 to here."

Evans smiled and pointed to Blake.

"Evans brought me a password or two," Blake said. "Spoiled my fun. I prefer hacking into a system. He made it too easy to get into the hotel system. The tenth-floor hallway monitor is running a continuous two-hour loop."

King still didn't feel safe. "So if a guy was monitoring it, he would have noticed he didn't see the rest of the team in the hallway when they came looking for Mundie.

"Kinger," MJ said. "Told you, Evans has our back. We had a drill just in case something like this happened."

Which told King that Evans knew something bad was a possibility. And that raised more questions for King, questions he couldn't seem to be able to ask.

Blake filled in for MJ. "I had it all set up ahead of time. Two quick commands just before pulling the plug in room 1010, and the loop went into play."

King walked to the window and back, trying to calm himself. He gave Evans a direct look. "What's going on?"

"Later," Evans said. "You're going to have to trust me on this. I thought, worst-case scenario, we could wait in this room for a while until everything was clear. But if a SWAT team apprehended Murphy, that changes everything. We need to get out there as soon as possible."

"Out where?" King said.

"When we get on the interstate," Evans said. "I'll have plenty of time to explain. But for now, you guys need to suit up."

Evans motioned for them to follow him to the bedroom off the main suite.

Laid out on the bed were four rubberized firefighter uniforms with helmets and boots and oxygen tanks.

"Cool," MJ said. "We *are* going to start a fire."

"Not quite," Evans said. "We're going to pull the alarm and toss smoke bombs down the stairwell. Once the fire trucks arrive, we'll join the confusion and get outside. I can arrange for another chopper to pick us up at the harbor."

Evans took another deep breath. "This is not an easy decision. It's going to scare a lot of people at the hotel and make life very inconvenient for them for the next few hours. But the stakes are too high…it has to be done."

CHAPTER 11

"Sir," the man behind the rental-car counter said to Evans, "your driver's license doesn't match the name on the credit card."

The man had slicked-back, thinning hair. He was slightly taller than Evans and much older. His voice carried clearly to King, who sat on a shiny red vinyl couch in the corner with MJ on one side and Blake on the other. King guessed that Evans was trying to use Mundie's government-issued Visa card for the rental.

With King beside him on the couch, MJ wasn't paying attention to the situation at the counter. "We could have kept the fire in control," he said.

"Huh?" Blake said.

"In the hotel room," MJ said. "My plan wasn't to burn down the entire room—just get enough of a fire going to draw some firemen in to rescue us."

King tried to concentrate on what was happening at the counter. Getting a car was crucial. Each second that passed was a second closer to Mundie following up on his threat to have every law enforcement officer in the state looking for them.

Escaping in the confusion of the smoke bomb was easy. Evans

had another chopper at the waterfront. Before letting them aboard the chopper, Evans had ordered them all to shut off their cell phones so they couldn't be tracked by GPS signals. After a short flight, Evans had put the chopper down at the Tacoma Narrows Airport, making the helicopter ride almost full circle for King. Directly south and west from the airport was Fox Island, in Puget Sound, and on the other side was McNeil Island. It had been a crazy couple of hours, King thought. In that time, King had lifted off from the road in front of his house, swooped into downtown Seattle, assaulted a CIA agent, and gone on the run nearly all the way back home with a second CIA agent. From where they were now, it was only a couple miles across the water to his home on the island.

"We would have been able to keep the fire under control," MJ said, elbowing King. "Easy. How could that have been dangerous?"

After landing in the chopper at the airport, the four of them had taken a five-minute taxi ride to the car-rental agency. Evans had asked King to give him Mundie's credit cards, and no other customers were at the counter. Not needing to wait had eased King's stress, but only a little. He expected a bunch of SWAT guys to surround them at any moment, just as they had done at the mobile home under drone surveillance.

More frustrating for King was that he hadn't had a chance to ask any questions. Not inside the chopper because of the engine noise, and not inside the taxi because the driver would have heard everything.

"And chances are with a fire alarm and firemen on the way," MJ said, "those four suit guys in the hallway would have bolted. So lighting a fire in the room was a good idea."

"You're right," King said to MJ. "I was wrong. A fire would have been a good idea."

King wanted to monitor what was happening at the counter, and MJ was too much of a distraction. The best way to get MJ to stop arguing was to agree with him. Otherwise, MJ would stay with it for hours.

"Knew it," MJ said, leaning back in satisfaction. "Absolutely knew it."

At the counter, Evans pulled out his CIA badge and held it in front of Slick-Back Hair.

"This isn't a situation I'm able to explain to someone without clearance," Evans said, leaving the badge on the counter. "But it won't take long to get that clearance. I'll give you a Washington, DC, phone number. Call in, give my boss your full name and birth date so he can put you into the system and confirm you are the person you say you are, working at this rental location. In turn, he'll give your new file a level-two clearance and also give you an authorization number to put on the rental agreement."

"Put me into the system?" Slick-Back said. "New file?"

"Not a big deal," Evans said. "It's some software thing. Pulls up everything about you. Goes through your Google search history, confirms that you're an upstanding citizen…that sort of thing." Evans paused. "You don't have any unpaid traffic violations, right? Taxes are fully paid? Nothing the Internal Revenue System would be interested in reviewing?"

As if on cue, a woman walked into the office with a pet poodle on a leash. Evans glanced back at her.

"Ma'am," he said. "I apologize if you're in a hurry. Looks like we need to put a call into DC and run some routine background checks before I can proceed with some business here. Might be a half hour. I'd be happy to arrange to get you some coffee while you wait. On the government's tab, of course."

To Slick-Back, Evans said, "I'll need you to disable the GPS tracker on the vehicle too. Once you get your level-two clearance, you'll understand why."

"A half hour?" she called to the counter, beginning to huff. "I don't have a half hour. I set this rental up three weeks ago!"

Evans turned to her. "Ma'am, could I have your name please?"

"My name? Why on earth would you—"

"Background check won't be necessary," Slick-Back broke in and told Evans. "We'll get this rental agreement printed out in about thirty seconds. You'll notice I've discounted the rate as a thank-you to our government. It shouldn't take long at all to disable the GPS tracker either."

Slick-Back spoke over Evans' shoulder to the woman. "Should be with you in less than a minute. Just need to get this gentlemen his car."

CHAPTER 12

In less than ten minutes, they were heading down the road.

"Have to make a call," Evans said. "To the front desk and make sure they send someone to untie Mundie. If he were to vomit for some reason, he'd suffocate."

As Evans made the call, King kept watching for swarms of police vehicles. He couldn't get Mundie's threat out of his mind. *"Because if you don't untie me, every law-enforcement officer in the state is going to be looking for you within the hour."*

After Evans finished the call, King let a few seconds of almost silent wind noise go by before speaking.

"My first question," King said, "is why Mundie picked me up, pretending you had sent him."

"You knew he was pretending?" Evans said.

"Mundie didn't give us the code phrase," Blake said. "You told us anyone who was part of the team would give us the code phrase. Mundie didn't."

"Yeah," MJ said, "so King snuck up behind him with a belt to use as a choke chain."

"Choke chain" brought bad memories to King. Dead Man's Switch memories. It reminded him of someone who had used a real choke chain on him, intending to take King to…

King forced away the thought, feeling a tightness in his chest return. He didn't want to deal with a panic attack here in the car.

"King?" Evans said, pulling King into the present.

"At my house, Mundie called me William, not King," King said. "That didn't seem right. Then he agreed with me that you like your coffee with two creams and two sugars. You hate it that way. All you drink is black."

"That's right," Evans said. "The blacker the better."

"Sir, is that a racist remark?" MJ asked. "I mean, what if I said the whiter the better? Wouldn't you be offended?"

King did a mental face-palm.

Then MJ said with triumph. "Wow. How about this awkward silence? One black or white joke is all it takes?"

"MJ," King said. "Really?"

They were best friends, but there were times when MJ could drive King nuts.

"Kinger," MJ said. "You must be losing a step, thinking I really meant what I said."

"Did not buy it," King said. A second later, King snorted. "Okay, I did. But it worked only because you're such a dork, it was an easy sell."

"Dang," Blake said. "I bought it too."

"Not me," Evans said. Then he laughed. "Okay, yeah, me too."

"Knew it," MJ said. "Absolutely knew it."

King gave it a few more beats and then asked, "So now that the comedy is out of the way, what's going on? What about what Mundie said in the hotel room?"

"About me conning you?" Evans answered. "I think it comes down to whether you believe me or him. He's saying what a rogue agent would say if I were the one tracking him down. And I'm saying what a rogue agent would say if he were the one tracking me down."

"We made our choice back in the hotel room," King said. "And I'm not second-guessing it. What I meant was what he said about every law-enforcement officer in the state coming after us."

"For starters," Evans answered, "we've probably used up our buffer of time. Not a bad move, trying to get him to think Volvo and that it's just the three of you on the run. So his next move is monitoring his credit card. And that will get him to the first car-rental place right away. He might even have agents moving in on it now."

Evans paused. "But here's why you don't have to worry. Mundie can't move openly on us. He's the rogue agent. All he has is his four guys. Or more—and that's why I can't make a play on him. We need to know how wide the corruption is and exactly what's going on with him."

"So," King said. "Mind telling me what you do know?"

CHAPTER 13

At midday, the sky was still cloudy, but the drizzle was gone, and Interstate 5 wasn't too crowded. If they jumped on it and headed north, they'd hit Canada in a few hours. Yes, King was interested in where Evans was taking them and even more interested in why. But most of all, he was interested in what Evans was saying right now.

"Sorry to Blake and MJ for repeating this," Evans said. "But we need to bring King up to speed. As an example, King, so you can understand where this got started, the LAPD has IAG."

Evans paused. "Sorry, I just get used to speaking in acronyms. The Los Angeles Police Department has its Internal Affairs Group. IAG is responsible to investigate the cops on the force. Someone makes a complaint, IAG is in place to make sure nobody inside the LAPD abuses police powers. Got it?"

"Got it," King said.

Evans was a focused driver. Never getting too close to the car in front, anticipating lane changes by other drivers, moving efficiently with the flow. It helped being in a new car like this Taurus.

Evans reached for the radio, turned it on, and told King, "Try to find a twenty-four-hour news station. Won't hurt to monitor things."

"Wish we could use our smartphones," Blake said. "There's a great police scanner app."

"I'm just being cautious," Evans said. "Everything should be cool. Police won't be looking for us."

When King found the news station, he turned down the volume and brought Evans back to the subject. "You were talking about IAG and the Los Angeles police. I'm guessing that what's happening with Mundie is the same?"

"Not quite," Evans said. "CIA doesn't quite have a division like that. I say not quite because yes, there are ways of investigating internal affairs for corruption or abuse, but by its nature, the organization is not transparent. Citizen complaints rarely come in against us."

"Or," King said with a grin, "you might threaten to put them at level-two clearance and have the IRS investigate their background?"

Evans gave King a quick glance and a quicker grin before turning his attention back to traffic. "Yeah, something like that. Thing is, a subtle threat like that only works on people with a guilty conscience."

Evans tapped the brake to make room for a semi driver who wasn't paying attention.

"Anyway," Evans continued as if nothing had happened, "the CIA does have an inspector general to keep things in line, and if someone really messed up, it would probably go to a congressional subcommittee devoted to overseeing the CIA. But really, that's not very effective. You need someone in the field to get at the truth. And that's where I come into this picture. I'm in the field, and someone is doing something wrong. But that someone can't know I'm looking into it, or that someone will disappear. With me so far?"

"With you," King said.

"So my boss—let's call him Smith—asked me if I would get involved in something that only he and I know about. Something off-the-books. When I agreed, he found some slush-fund money and set me loose. Part of the agreement was that I couldn't let anyone know I'd been authorized. The political fallout would be disastrous. Still with me?"

"Buckled in," King said. "And still with you."

"The three of you are as off-the-books as anything. I thought it would be perfect. High school guys, no connections, no records, but with the expertise I needed for the first stage, which was to track down someone through cyberspace—a minor actor in all of this. That's what I sold your parents on, and they agreed it would be safe. It should have been routine."

"Minor actor?" King said. "And the major actor?"

"What I need to find out," Evans said, "is if Ron Delamarre is guilty as charged, or if someone else in the—"

For King, it was a delayed reaction. "Ron Delamarre!"

"Yeah. That Ron Delamarre. Software billionaire. Indicted on terrorism charges. Fled the country. Wanted by Interpol."

"Wow," King said. "Heavy stuff."

"It gets better—or worse, depending on your perspective. There's some murky stuff that I don't want to explain because, really, you don't have the clearance. But there may or may not be a faction within the CIA that's been putting a squeeze play on Delamarre for a top-secret software thing that Delamarre may or may not possess and that Delamarre may or may not have stolen. Regardless, there's a terrible chance that a faction of a few connected agents have gone rogue within the CIA. We don't know enough to identify them, just that rumors exist."

"And," King said, "that Ron Delamarre has been charged with something related to terrorism and is on the run."

"That about sums it up," Evans said.

"Except for the fact that Blake and MJ and I are in a car with you after assaulting an agent who pretended to be bringing me in to meet with you."

"Except for that," Evans said. "My best guess is that he wanted all three of you together to contain the situation and find out what was going on. That's what really scares me. Somehow, it seems, someone else in the organization has wind of this. They knew where to find you guys, they knew you were involved, and they took down our main witness—Jack Murphy, the guy in the mobile home—who the prosecution wasn't supposed to know would testify that Ron Delamarre wasn't a terrorist."

Evans signaled and eased two lanes to the right.

Evans said, "Blake? MJ?"

MJ took the lead. "Kinger, Evans went to our parents and asked if we could become cyber bounty hunters and help him find a guy. Someone who was on the run for missing child-support payments. It was a piece of cake for us."

"By 'us,'" King said to MJ, half turning so he could look directly into the backseat, "you mean you let Blake help you a little."

Blake grinned and said nothing. Blake's computer and programming skills were undisputed.

"I ordered pizza when he was hungry," MJ said. "Important job. And offered emotional support."

"That," Blake said, "plus he's older than I am. My parents weren't going to let me work with Evans unless I had company. And since you had stomach issues, MJ had to be the one."

Stomach issues. *Right,* King thought. *How about panic-attack issues?*

"I assured your parents this was a simple job," Evans said. "Except for my boss, I was the only one who knew about the hotel room, the computer work, and the drone. At least, I thought I was."

"Safe conclusion then that Mundie works for the rogue faction?" King asked. "How did they find out what was happening off the books?"

King saw Evans tighten his jaw.

"That's one thing I need to find out," Evans said. "But my bigger priority is that I have to get you guys clear and back to your parents as soon as possible with no collateral damage."

"Right," King said, wondering why Evans hadn't called their parents yet. Or offered to take them to McNeil Island.

CHAPTER 14

"Our lucky day," Evans said, glancing ahead to the side of the freeway. He pointed. "Look at that."

Two panhandlers were standing beside a sign marking an off-ramp. Both wore army-surplus clothing and had heavy beards. One held up a sign handwritten on cardboard. "Time machine ran out of gas. Need money to go back in time and stop Justin Bieber."

The other man's sign was also handwritten. "No bills larger than $50 after 8 p.m."

Evans pulled onto the shoulder and put the Taurus in park. He hit the electric window on King's side, and both men wandered over.

King wished the breeze was blowing in the opposite direction. It came into the car, bringing with it the smell of men who hadn't showered in days or maybe even weeks.

"Men," Evans said to them. "These boys with me are too young to drive. Either of you have a driver's license? I need help picking up a vehicle, and I have two hundred dollars for you if you can help out."

The first guy burped and patted his back pocket. "Sure, I got a driver's license. Just forgot to bring it with me."

"Good enough," Evans said. "I'll give you a hundred bucks now to get in the car. We'll go pick up the other car, and then you can follow me in this one. When we get the second car to my house, I'll bring you back here."

"How long is it gonna take?" the second one said. "I got things to do, places to go. Two hundred bucks doesn't get you that much of my time."

"Half hour," Evans said. "That work for you?"

The first guy winced. "Work. Don't say that word."

The second guy shook his "No bills larger than $50 after 8 p.m." sign and said, "I'm good with it. Don't matter how you pay us. Not even close to eight p.m. yet."

Evans handed a smartphone to King and spoke in a low voice. "Google me another car-rental agency. Then call ahead and rent a car under the name Lucas Thompson. Try to find something as close by as possible. It's going to be crowded when those two get in the car."

And smelly, King thought. It gave him a whole new level of sympathy for Mundie and the unwashed sock King had shoved into the man's mouth.

CHAPTER 15

Three hours earlier, King had been in his mother's workshop, at peace and safe from the world. All that had changed with bewildering speed, but King still wasn't in a position to ask questions about what was going on. Not stuck in the middle of the front seat, pressed against Evans on one side and panhandler number one on the other.

In the backseat, Blake was stuck in the middle with MJ to his left and panhandler number two on the other.

King breathed through his mouth, keeping his teeth together so he wouldn't be obvious. He realized he should be grateful. What was happening was a distraction from any sense of panic. On the other hand, the body odor filling the car was so intense, even a panic attack would have been more comfortable.

Mercifully, they reached the second car-rental agency in less than two minutes.

Evans pulled into the parking lot. He opened Mundie's wallet and pulled out five twenties.

"Here," he said, reaching across King to give it to the guy on the other side. "Hundred up front."

The guy grabbed it and then counted. "Yup. Hundred."

"I'm going to write down an address," Evans said. "Instead of following me there, leave now and drop off the car sometime tomorrow at that address. I'll throw in an extra forty for cab fare, and you can take a taxi from there to wherever you need to go."

"Forty ain't enough," the guy in the backseat said. "Tomorrow, we're supposed to be at my sister's house."

"Where does she live?" Evans asked.

"Spokane," the first guy said.

"Portland," the second guy said at the same time.

"Hey," Evans said, "you sure I should believe you about this sister? How do I know you're not just trying to scam some extra money from me?"

"He's got one sister lives in Spokane," the first guy said. "I didn't know the sister he was supposed to visit was the other one who lives in…"

"Portland," the second guy said. "That's the one we need to visit. Gonna cost at least another hundred to get there."

Evans peeled off more twenties. "As long as you promise to bring the car to the address I give you before you go visit her. Not after. I'll be checking the odometer when I get this car back."

"Yeah, yeah," the first guy said. "You can depend on us."

"And you have a valid driver's license?" Evans asked.

"Of course," the first guy said.

"Then we should be good," Evans said. "The car is yours. Make sure you drive careful and leave it in the same shape it's in now."

"Except for gas," the second guy said. "Don't expect us to put in gas to fill it up again."

CHAPTER 16

King turned down the volume on the radio. The announcers were at the top of the hour, on a third set of the cycled news. Not much in the headlines they had not heard yet.

They'd been driving over an hour, now headed east on Interstate 90, nearly through the mountains.

MJ broke the silence. "Evans, I've been giving this a lot of thought. I know you did your best, but I'm pretty sure those two panhandlers scammed you about the rental car. New car, full tank of gas, a bunch of money…I can't see anything good happening. My dad says a lot of panhandlers don't spend their money that wisely. That's why he gives to local charities instead. He keeps copies of the receipts and gives them to panhandlers instead of money. That way they know he really does want to help people like them. And that thing about a sister. I didn't believe it for a second. I think they were just trying to get more money out of you."

King did another mental face-palm at MJ's remark. King had been at the counter of the second rental-car agency when Evans had tossed down a driver's license with his photo and the name Lucas Thompson on it and a credit card to match. Fake identification was probably a breeze for someone in the CIA. Evans clearly wanted to make sure nobody could track them. Renting a car with Mundie's credit card was a sure way to get pursuers looking for the Ford Taurus instead of their new set of wheels—a gray Dodge Charger. Letting a couple of panhandlers take the Taurus on a joyride that might last for days was a perfect way to keep Mundie looking in the wrong places.

With a smile that suggested he enjoyed MJ's innocence and lack of street smarts, Evans said, "MJ, sometimes you have to believe the best about people and give them a chance."

"Sir," MJ said, "you also have to be realistic. I would think someone like you who has to chase down bad guys would know that. My dad says—"

"MJ," Evans said. "Now that you mention it, you're probably right. Maybe those guys were lying about their sister. Maybe they won't deliver the car tomorrow like they promised."

"Knew it," MJ said. "Absolutely knew it."

That told King that Evans also knew that MJ would argue something for hours and that it was easier to just agree.

Time to rescue Evans with a subject change.

"Evans," King said, "I have a quick question, only because I'm nervous. Have you noticed a black Escalade behind us? It's been there almost since we crossed the pass at Snoqualmie."

"Yes," Evans said from behind the steering wheel, looking as fresh and as alert as when they'd left the second rental-car agency in the Charger. "I've been watching it."

"Looks like some kind of official vehicle. You know, like the ones in presidential motorcades. Or an unmarked state patrol vehicle."

"I've been watching it. There's nothing to worry about. Trust me."

King surveyed his side-view mirror again. The Escalade had been behind them for about a half hour. That raised his stress level despite Evans' assurance. He also kept expecting to see a convoy of state troopers in patrols cars, lights flashing, whipping toward them.

Then he glanced ahead, expecting to see a road stop with cars funneling into a single lane so state troopers could check vehicles for passengers.

King had been fighting this anticipatory dread since getting into the Charger. The Snoqualmie Pass had taken them to the summit of the Cascade Mountains, and descending at just over the speed limit on I-90, they were now reaching a sign that said Ellensburg was ten miles down the road. Evans had had little more to report, so there had been lots of silence—except when Evans had explained to them what a rain shadow was, and that was just to keep MJ from breaking the silences with new knock-knock jokes.

That's how King had learned that a rain shadow was the dry area on the side of a mountain away from the wind. On the other side, prevailing winds forced moist air up the mountain, and as the air rose and cooled, the moisture condensed and turned into rain or snow. Then as the wind dropped down the rain-shadow side of the mountain, it was clear of moisture.

King was able to see the effects on the descent. Vegetation had changed from thick, green, and dense to lighter, sporadic, and browner as they moved into the rain shadow of the mountains. Barely sixty miles behind them was McNeil Island, wet and fog shrouded. Ahead was the semiarid stretch that would reach all the way to Spokane. All that Evans had said was that they needed to get to the mobile home, isolated somewhere in the desert between here and the next range of mountains.

"Knock, knock," MJ said.

"Please," Evans responded, "this time, no one answer the door."

"Knock, knock," MJ said.

Silence.

"Last one," MJ said. "I'll keep knocking until someone answers."

Silence.

"Knock, knock," MJ said.

Silence.

"Knock, knock," MJ said.

Silence.

"Knock, knock," MJ said.

"Urrgh," Evans said. Irritating as MJ could be, King did find it funny. But if he laughed, MJ would spend another five hours coming up with knock-knock jokes. It was also funny because King had seen Evans in a few tense life-or-death situations already, and he assumed those hadn't been the only ones for Evans. During those situations, Evans had shown nothing but patience and calm. MJ, however, had been able to get through Evans' protective shell. But then, that was MJ.

"Knock, knock," MJ said.

"Who's there?" Evans said, not hiding his exasperation.

"Dwayne," MJ said.

Evans sighed. "Dwayne who?"

"Dwayne the bathtub," MJ said. "It's overflowing!"

MJ cackled in triumph as Evans groaned. King bit his lip to keep from smiling. Better to listen to knock-knocks jokes than to worry about when another panic attack might hit. Or worry about an unmarked state patrol vehicle following a couple hundred yards behind.

"Knock, knock," Blake said.

"Blake!" Evans said. "Not you too! Not my socially awkward computer genius model of perfect politeness!"

"Knock, knock," Blake said.

"Who's there?" Evan said, now smiling.

"Noah," Blake answered.

"Noah who?" Evans said.

"Noah good place we can get something to eat?"

When Evans laughed, King joined in. Not MJ.

"How fair is that?" MJ said. "Thirty of my best knock-knock jokes, and all I get are the sound of crickets out of an audience that might not even be alive. Blake tells one and brings down the house."

"We're hungry," King said. "That's why. It's all about timing."

"I'll show you timing," MJ said. Which made no sense to King. But he figured he'd better laugh, or MJ would keep trying. So King laughed.

"That's better," MJ said. "We going to eat soon?"

"Ellensburg," Evans said. "We need to find a phone store. Lucas Thompson is going to run in and get a couple of smartphones."

"Lucas Thompson?" MJ asked.

"One of my fully supported identifications," Evans said. "We need Internet connection, and it would be stupid to use any of our own phones. Mundie would track us down in minutes."

The mention of Mundie brought down the mood. For a moment, they'd forgotten that they were on the run from rogue CIA agents.

"While I'm getting the phones under the name of Lucas Thompson," Evans said, "hopefully we'll see a place you guys can grab some fast food. King, dig some cash out of Mundie's wallet. Keep the receipts so we can reimburse the CIA when this is cleared up. And then—"

Evans stopped and turned up the volume on the radio. The announcer was speaking louder in an excited voice.

"...On the lookout for one black male adult and three white juvenile males. Wanted for a bank robbery attempt and a shooting of innocent bystanders during the robbery. They are traveling in a gray Dodge Charger, license number..."

King felt cold clutch at his heart as the announcer read the numbers. He didn't have to do it, but did it anyway. He reached into the glove compartment for the rental agreement and saw that the numbers matched.

"Once again," the announcer said, "consider these wanted men to be armed and dangerous. If you see an adult black male and three white juveniles in a gray Dodge Charger with that license number, call the state police at this number. Do not approach the vehicle."

The announcer began to give out the 800 number for the state police.

"What!" MJ shouted. "Blake, hit the floor so no one sees us!"

King saw them slide down and disappear from view. Their move attracted a look from a woman in a Volkswagen Jetta passing them in the left lane. She looked again, and then a weird look of comprehension filled her face.

Great, King thought. His throat began to tighten. But this was natural fear, not the beginning of a full-blown panic attack.

Evans spoke calmly. "I was afraid Mundie might do something like that. But I didn't want you guys to have to worry about it until it actually happened."

"I'm plenty worried now," MJ said from the floor of the backseat.

King noticed that the woman in the Jetta had grabbed her cell phone. But that was the least of his worries. He also noticed that the black Escalade had closed the gap.

"Evans," King said, trying to keep his voice as calm as Evans' had been, "you see the Escalade behind us, right?"

"And the flashing lights," Evans answered.

Sure enough, the Escalade had a light bar inside the interior, and it was now flashing red and blue. The headlights alternated on and off, adding to the visibility of the pursuing vehicle.

"Hang on," Evans said. "This could get dicey."

He floored the accelerator and roared past the woman in the Jetta, with the Escalade roaring to keep up.

CHAPTER 17

Thirty seconds later, a sign indicated an exit a half mile ahead. With the speedometer pushing 90, and rushing past the few cars that were in the right lane, Evans eased off on the gas and put on his signal light to exit.

"This is not smart," Evans said. He moved into the right lane. "I've never been a fan of high-speed pursuits, and I don't want to see anyone get hurt."

Blake and MJ were sitting up again. There was no need to hide from the cops when one was directly behind them, siren now wailing.

"I don't want to see anyone hurt either," MJ said. "So go faster. If we get pulled over and thrown in jail, my mom is going to put some serious hurt on me."

"That woman in the Jetta," Evans said to King, ignoring MJ's plea, "the one who looked like she was calling us in—did she put her cell phone down?"

King glanced across Evans through the driver's side window and caught the woman staring at them with happy excitement on her face as she began to pass them again.

"Phone down," King said. "She looked smug, like she's glad a cop got us."

"Excellent," Evans said. "She was a witness I thought could get us in trouble."

The exit came up fast. Evans took the off-ramp, reaching the stop sign at a crossroad. The right-hand turn would take them on a straight road, leading toward flat, open fields with irrigation systems. Left, it crossed back over the interstate and wound upward into some hills, disappearing around a curve about a quarter mile away.

King craned his head to look behind them. The Escalade was directly on their bumper.

Instead of pulling over onto the shoulder, however, Evans paused briefly at the stop sign to make sure it was clear of cross traffic and then turned left and accelerated gradually toward the hills.

"Any other witnesses on the interstate are long past us now," Evans said. "Time to hide."

He gunned it again with the Escalade in pursuit.

"Dude," MJ said. "You rock! Thank you! Thank you! You have no idea how scary my mom can be."

Blake put his hands over his face.

King kept an eye on the Escalade. He was surprised to see the flashing lights shut down. Same with the alternating headlights.

He was also surprised when Evans stopped his acceleration at the speed limit.

From there, the pursuit was leisurely. The Escalade kept a healthy distance and maintained the same speed as Evans as both vehicles followed the contours of the land on the winding road. As they ascended, more and more trees began to fill in the open areas.

"Um," King said, "isn't it a safe assumption that this guy is radioing for backup?"

"Huh," Evans said. "That was a polite way of suggesting I need to think this through, wasn't it."

"Yeah," King said. "It was."

Evans kept driving.

"No other response to my polite suggestion?" King said.

"Sure," Evans said. "Keep your eyes open for a good spot to ditch this vehicle. We need a turnoff with lots of trees to screen the car from the road. When we abandon it, we don't want it found for a while."

"Um, just as a polite suggestion," MJ said, "I'd like to point out that if you expect us to dash out of the car and outrun this guy, his bullets will be faster than my feet."

Evans chuckled. "Good point, MJ. Let's try this instead. After I stop, you get out of the car, go to his window, and politely ask if we could get a ride back to the interstate and on to Ellensburg. Point out that the four of us need to get some throwaway cell phones and some food."

"Good one, sir," MJ said.

"Or," Evans said, "maybe I could try a knock-knock joke."

MJ began to moan. "My mom is going to kill me."

"There," King said to Evans, pointing ahead. "To the right. Dirt road with trees on both sides."

"Perfect." Evans began to slow. He signaled for the turn.

"Seriously?" MJ said. "A turn signal?"

King glanced back. The Escalade slowed and put on a right-hand signal light as well.

Evans turned onto the dirt road. He drove slowly with branches and weeds reaching out from both sides of the dirt road. The Escalade followed but didn't close the distance until Evans stopped a minute down the dirt road.

Evans hit the power button to roll down his window and shut off the engine. The Escalade stopped at their back bumper.

A cheerful sound of chirping birds reached the interior of the car when the motor of the Escalade shut down.

"We're trapped," MJ said. "And I may have just peed myself."

A tall man wearing jeans, a jean jacket, and a cowboy hat stepped out of the Escalade. He reached the car and peered through the driver's window at everyone inside. The man's face was thin. He had a graying mustache. Looked like a sheriff from an old Western. He had a weathered face, and spiderwebs of wrinkles showed he was probably ten years older than Evans.

"I have reason to believe that this car and you people are wanted for an armed bank robbery," Sheriff Guy said. "One black adult male and three white juveniles, if the report is correct. Vehicle and license plate also match the description. Perhaps you could all get out of the vehicle?"

"Knock-knock," Evans said.

"Pardon me?" Sheriff Guy said.

"Take me away," MJ said to no one in particular. "Please. Just get this over with and take me away now."

"The kid in the backseat loves knock-knock jokes, so I thought I'd treat you to one," Evans said to Sheriff Guy. Patient in tone. "Knock, knock."

"Okay," Sheriff Guy answered. "Who's there?"

"Police," Evans said.

"Police who?"

"Police give us a ride into town," Evans said. "We need some cell phones, and the boys here are hungry."

MJ bent over and shoved his right hand into his mouth to keep himself from screaming in anguish.

Sheriff Guy looked at MJ and said, "Hey, the joke wasn't that bad."

Then Sheriff Guy looked at Evans. "Think this is my first rodeo? I already picked up some throwaway cell phones, and I also packed a picnic basket with food for a couple days. So how about we get this show on the road?"

CHAPTER 18

The Escalade had three rows of seats, but the third row, in the back, was flat because the rear compartment was filled with what looked to King like metal detectors. As he slid into the middle row with MJ and Blake, he did a quick count.

Five.

Five metal detectors. Dull army green. Long handles, circles at the bottom.

King didn't have a chance to ask about them because Evans clicked on his seat belt in the front passenger seat and spoke as Sheriff Guy began to reverse the vehicle. "This is my friend Bill Moore. We were on a SEAL team together a long time ago. He went his way and joined a security detail for the state governor. I was recruited by the CIA for Special Ops. Bill's one of the best, and he's got our back."

King was on the driver's side of the middle row. Blake was in the middle because he was the smallest, and MJ was directly behind Evans.

MJ said, "Might have been nice to know that earlier. You know, about the time he turned on the flashing lights and before I peed my pants?"

King was glad MJ hadn't really peed his pants. But he understood the sentiment.

"Bad habit for which I apologize," Evans said. "Secrets are currency in the intelligence community. Doesn't take much time in the business before you start parceling out information on a need-to-know basis."

MJ began, "I would have needed to know he was a good guy. That could have prevented some serious scare on my part."

Evans laughed. He obviously liked MJ. "And unfortunately, I'm the one deciding what's need-to-know."

"Like when you called Mr. Moore at the service station without telling us?" King asked Evans. Evans had apologized for needing a bathroom break about fifteen minutes into the trip.

Moore spoke up. "Call me Moore. Not Mr. Moore, okay? Everyone calls me Moore. It throws me off to hear the 'Mister.'"

"Told you they're sharp," Evans said to Moore. "King knew we had all our cell phones shut down, so there was only one place and time I could have reached you—when I made an excuse to stop at a truck stop."

That's exactly what King had decided. No way could Evans have foreseen the morning's events and set this up before Mundie took King off McNeil Island.

"Keep going," Evans told King. "I use a pay phone at the back of the truck stop..."

"You tell him what we're driving and where we're headed," King said. "I'm guessing Mr....I'm guessing Moore must have been in Seattle when you reached him. That would have given him a straight, short run east on I-90 while we were coming up the longer way from Tacoma on Highway 18."

"I made it to Price Creek Rest Area at mile marker 61, just east of Snoqualmie Pass," Moore said. "I parked on the exit ramp going in. If Evans didn't see me there, the backup was for him to take another rest stop and delay till I showed up."

"King picked you up almost right away when you got back on the interstate," Evans said to Moore. "Maybe you need to take a refresher course on tailing targets."

"Humph," Moore said.

"You were anticipating that Mundie might actually call in law enforcement to look for us, right?" King asked Evans. "That's why you kept the news radio on?"

"Yes," Evans said. "I decided that was need-to-know too. I didn't wanted you guys stressed out more than you were. Moore and I had also decided to push as far as we could in both vehicles before dumping the rental. The farther out from Tacoma, the bigger the circle to search."

"So when the fake bank-robbery warrant was announced," Moore said, "I knew it was time to make my move. Anyone seeing the Charger on the interstate would think I'm arresting you. Now, with the rental car hidden, there's little chance we'll be found."

"That's pretty much it," Evans said.

By then, Moore had finished the awkward process of turning the vehicle around. He moved away from the rental and headed out the dirt road and back toward the interstate.

"Except for the metal detectors in the back," Blake said. "We're headed to Jack Murphy's mobile home, right?"

"Why guess that?" Evans answered.

"Metal detectors in the back," MJ said.

King said, "MJ, he was asking how Blake knew our destination would be the Jack Murphy location."

"Knew it," MJ said. "Absolutely knew it."

Blake said to Evans, "We're headed that direction, for starts. But if it had been about just arresting Jack Murphy, you would have done that the day we found him for you. Instead, you had MJ and me put Jack Murphy on surveillance. Now I understand why. You were hoping we'd see him go out on his property for whatever you want us to detect. Which means the team that arrested him has no idea that there's something else that needs to be found."

"You're right," Moore said to Evans. "They are sharp. Very sharp. Good team you've put together."

"That leaves an obvious question," MJ said. "What are we looking for?"

"A tunnel entrance," Evans said.

King waited for more explanation, but it didn't come. So he asked the next obvious question. "What's in the tunnel?"

Evans turned to look back at all three of them. The Escalade was almost back to the winding highway that would lead to the interstate.

"Gentlemen, you're going to have to trust me on this one," Evans said. "We're looking for something that is crucial for national security. What's inside is on a need-to-know basis, and you three don't have the clearance for it."

He paused as Moore swung onto the highway.

"Trust me on this too," Evans continued. "It's in your best interests not to know."

CHAPTER 19

Cruising down the interstate gave King a chance to mentally review what he knew about the three days when MJ and Blake had been cyber bounty hunters for Evans.

During the first few hours of the trip, between stupid knock-knock jokes from MJ, Evans and Blake and MJ had put it together in pieces for King.

Evans had first approached the parents of all three, asking permission for the three to help track down Jack Murphy, a man who had failed to make child-support payments.

Evans had used a few arguments with the parents. One, the boys would get paid, so it was summer employment. Two, they were on a summer break, so they wouldn't miss school. Three, it was routine cyber work with no danger—a chance for Blake to use his white-hat hacking skills while MJ and King learned extra computer skills. Four, Evans was short staffed because his own computer people were focused on higher-priority national security issues. Five, while Evans couldn't reveal why, there were national security reasons for needing to locate Jack Murphy, so in short, King and MJ and Blake would be serving their country.

The parents had seen no danger and no reason not to help Evans. King, fighting panic attacks, had used illness as an excuse not to leave the island.

After assaulting Mundie and fleeing the hotel with the others, he learned how easy it had been for Blake to find Jack Murphy's location.

Armed with the man's Social Security number and other information supplied by Evans, Blake had tracked down Jack Murphy within hours to a site in Washington State's Yakima River Valley between the towns of Ellensburg to the north and Yakima to the south.

Evans had put other things in motion, including the authorization for a military drone with a high-power camera to watch Murphy's mobile home. During the day, it was visual surveillance. At night, infrared.

That's when MJ had become a valuable resource. Blake and MJ spent day and night, alternating shifts, in constant real-time monitoring of the aerial view of the mobile home with instructions to call Evans the instant Jack Murphy stepped outside.

Nothing had happened until King and Mundie entered the hotel room. Then Mundie's SWAT team had appeared. Once he had King and Blake and MJ contained in one place, it was time for Jack Murphy to be apprehended too.

One phase of Mundie's plan had been successful. At least, it was assumed to be successful. The drone had been blown from the sky before it could record Jack Murphy's arrest, but Evans concluded that Murphy would not have been able to escape.

Evans also concluded that Mundie must have somehow had an inside track on what Blake and MJ were doing because he knew enough about it to find King and pretend that Evans had sent him to get King. But Evans had no idea how Mundie could have learned about the entire off-the-books operation in the first place.

That was essentially all King had known until Moore showed up in the black Escalade. Now, with the rented Dodge Charger in a place unlikely to be found for days, and in a government-sanctioned vehicle from the governor's security detail, they seemed to have gained some freedom for a while.

King was willing to accept that they didn't have the clearance to know what might be in some tunnels that might be on Murphy's property. But he did have an important question.

He waited until they'd unpacked lunches and everyone was eating as they drove. Then King spoke in a quiet voice. "Evans, Mundie obviously made up a fake report about a bank robbery just to get the police to look for us."

"I figured there was an even-even chance he'd go that far," Evans said. "I thought he'd probably want this to stay as off-the-books as possible. But I guess he wasn't bluffing in the hotel room."

"Probably found out about our Dodge Charger by locating the original rental," King said.

"Yeah," Evans said. "I was hoping to buy a little more time by setting those panhandlers loose with it. But I'm guessing the rental-car guy didn't disable the GPS like he promised. Once Mundie tracked down the panhandlers in the first car, they would have given him the location of the second car-rental place. I wasn't too worried though because Moore and I had this backup plan in place. We were going to switch vehicles up ahead anyway."

"So as it stands," King said, "Blake and MJ and I have assaulted a CIA officer and have been publicly charged with participating in an armed bank robbery."

"First chance I get," Evans said, "I'll call your parents and tell them not to worry. Moore's going to break out our new cell phones right away."

"Our parents are going to ask you the same question I have," King said.

"Fire away," Evans said.

"How do we resolve this? We *did* assault a CIA officer."

"It gets resolved," he answered, "when we get enough leverage on Mundie for him to make the charges disappear."

"Leverage?" MJ said with a mouthful of submarine sandwich.

"We assemble the evidence to show he is a rogue agent with his own agenda," Evans said. "We take that to the top of the CIA. That will justify everything about this off-the-books operation."

Moore spoke. He wasn't eating but instead drove with textbook safety, two miles an hour above the speed limit. Eyes on the road. Both hands relaxed in the proper position on the steering wheel.

"Boys," Moore said. "It's simple. If you want to avoid jail time, we need to find those tunnels."

CHAPTER 20

The mobile home was perched on a plateau overlooking the Yakima River. To reach it, Moore had continued on Interstate 90 east, past the two Ellensburg exits, and turned south on Interstate 82, which led to Yakima. But after only a few minutes on 82, Moore had taken an exit for a crossroad west again to link up with Highway 821, a secondary road that followed the Yakima River.

They had headed south with the river to their right. The highway followed the snaking course of the river so closely that often the water was only a stone's throw away. Occasionally they could see rafters enjoying the water in the heat. There was no trace of the drizzle they'd left behind because of the rain shadow cast by the Cascade mountains, which were visible during the short stretches of highway that rose out of the river canyon. The land between the river and the highway was green with trees and bushes that could tap into the water source, but east of the highway, the land was gray and brown, dominated by the sagebrush and tufted grass that King had seen in the hotel room on the surveillance of the mobile home.

About twenty minutes after they left the interstate, the canyon had widened, showing irrigated land on the floodplain between the highway and the river. Just past that, Moore had turned left onto a gravel road that wound out of the canyon and up to the mobile home, which was set high enough to provide a view of Mount Rainer on the western horizon.

Moore shut off the engine and swung open his door. Hot, dry wind whistled through the Escalade when Evans opened the door on the other side.

Evans unbuckled his seat belt.

"Mr. Evans," Blake said, "I'm feeling really weird. Dizzy. Like I'm going to fall over if I stand up. It happens every couple of weeks. At home, my mom makes me lie down in my bedroom and shuts the curtains. It's not a big deal really, nothing to worry about. But could I..."

"We'll be okay," Evans said. "The four of us can start sweeping the grounds."

"Thanks," Blake said.

"I'll leave the engine running so you don't get hot," Moore said. He leaned in, turned on the ignition, and then shut the door.

To Evans, Moore said, "Let's make sure the dwelling is clear first."

He meant the mobile home. It looked as if it had been built in the 1960s. It had a sagging roof, and the metal siding was a blurred gray except for spots where new siding had been put in place to patch it. Streaks of rust showed where rivets held the patches in place. The steps leading up to a leaning front porch were rickety, and the screen door hung at an angle. The satellite dish at the far end, however, looked brand-new.

King went out his side from the middle row, MJ the other side.

King shut the door and noted with satisfaction that the smoked-glass windows made it impossible to see inside.

MJ came around to King's side. They watched the mobile home and waited for Moore and Evans, who went inside with drawn pistols.

"This is real," MJ said.

"This is real," King said.

"Also hot," MJ said.

"At least it's a dry heat," King said.

"Maybe I need a dizzy spell to keep me inside the vehicle," MJ said.

"He doesn't have a dizzy spell," King said quietly. "There was a pencil in the pouch in front of me. I used part of the sandwich wrapper to slip him a note to come up with an excuse to stay inside with his laptop and use the hotspot to grab an Internet connection. We need him to find a way into some personnel files and to do some research on Evans and Mundie and Moore."

MJ's eyes opened wide. "For what?"

The lack of an explanation about why they were looking for a tunnel had been nagging at King, but he felt as if he didn't have much choice but to follow directions.

"That's the thing," King said. "Something is really bothering me about this. I don't know if we can trust Evans. And if we can't, this is a bad place to be with him."

CHAPTER 21

When Moore and Evans returned, they didn't need to tell King and MJ that the mobile home was clear. Because if it wasn't clear, they wouldn't be returning with their pistols back in their shoulder holsters.

In fact, nothing around the mobile home suggested that earlier that day it had been swarmed by SWAT guys. Nothing but sand, clumps of grass, sagebrush, the mobile home, and a power line that led to the rear of the home.

"That's an expensive suit," Moore said to Evans. "Brought you some coveralls. And some boots. They're in the back."

"Thanks." Evans went to the rear of the vehicle and raised the liftgate.

While they were waiting for Evans to change, Moore had a question for King and MJ. "Second of four American presidents to have been assassinated?"

"James A. Garfield," King said.

"Knew it," MJ chimed. "Absolutely knew it."

"Inventor of the telephone?" Moore asked.

King gave MJ a chance to answer, and when MJ casually looked away as if he were interested in a hawk soaring over the canyon, King answered again. "Alexander Graham Bell."

"Knew it," MJ said. "Absolutely knew it."

"What do the two have in common?" Moore asked.

King was stumped.

MJ said, "The doctors couldn't find the bullet in Garfield. Alexander Graham Bell fabricated a primitive metal detector. But it was foiled because they forgot Garfield was laying on a mattress with metal springs, which was also a new invention."

Moore applauded MJ.

That was one of the things about MJ. He played the role of clown so well, you never knew when he was pretending not to be smart. He'd once told King that his childhood dream had been to become a ballerina, and he'd said it with such straight-faced melancholy that King still didn't know whether it was true or MJ was messing with him.

There was only one thing for King to say at this moment, so he said it. "Knew it. Absolutely knew it."

"Enough of the history lesson," Evans said, poking out his head from behind the vehicle. "Come here."

They did.

Evans first passed out pairs of leather-palmed gardening gloves to each of them. Then he pulled out the metal detectors, handing one to Moore, the next to MJ, the third to King, and keeping the fourth. "These are MD4s. American military uses them in Afghanistan to sweep for victim-operated switches."

MJ echoed him. "Victim-operated switches."

"Fancy name for booby traps," Evans explained. "Step on the switch, and boom. Most land mines are made with as much plastic as possible to avoid detection. But these detect the small metal portion of a land mine's switch."

"Except," Moore said in a tone as dry as the wind, "for the land mines that are triggered by nearby vibrations or movement or sound or trip wires."

"Just to be clear," MJ said, "we *are* looking for tunnels. Not land mines."

"Hope so," Moore said.

"Hope?" MJ's voice trembled.

Moore laughed. "Jumpy one, aren't you."

"I usually just pee my pants instead of jump," MJ said. "Today, I should have worn Pampers."

Moore laughed again. "Evans, I can see why you wanted this guy on the team."

Then Moore turned serious. "Picture a vertical shaft going down about ten feet to a level tunnel. The shaft will likely be circular, so the lid will be like a manhole cover. Even if it's square, it will probably be made of plastic, but the screws will be metal. You'll be wearing headsets, and these detectors are as sensitive as anything made. If the screws are there, you'll find them."

Moore waited for questions. There were none.

What King wanted to ask was what might be in the tunnel, if it was here. And how it might save them. But Evans had made it clear that this was a national security issue.

"Sand like this is perfect for covering up a lid," Moore said, kicking at the ground. Wind took away a small cloud. "Just shovel about six inches of sand over it, let the wind blow for a few minutes, and it looks like part of the landscape. You wouldn't find it even if you stepped on it. At least, not without our metal detectors. So Evans and I will set up grids."

Moore waved his own detector. "Overlap your sweeps so you don't miss any ground." He made side-to-side motions with the dinner-plate-sized coil at the end of the handle and continued giving instructions. "Make sure you keep the coil parallel to the ground. Don't tilt it, or it will lose its sensitivity."

Moore looked at Evans, and Evans handed Moore his metal detector and slipped on his pair of gardening gloves.

Evans stepped to a tuft that was nearby. "See the serrated edges? It's a way for the grass to protect itself from grazing animals. You'll need the gloves."

He bent over and grabbed a tuft and pulled. The grass didn't yank free.

Evans straightened. "Dry climate like this, the grasses grow in clumps like this and send roots down as far as six feet to try to find moisture. Good luck pulling them loose."

He made a gesture with his hands to take in the land around the mobile home. "We've got hundreds and hundreds of clumps. It's easy to hide a tunnel entrance with a fake clump and sand to hold it in place. So don't forget to sweep the clumps. If you get a beep, tug on the clump. If the clump comes up fast, it's fake, and you know you've found what we need. Any questions?"

King shook his head no. MJ did the same.

"Okay," Moore said. "Give me and Evans a few minutes to set up the grid. Once you two get started, he and I are going to do a more thorough search of the mobile home. We'll come out and help with the tunnel search as soon as possible. Clear?"

"Clear," MJ said.

"Clear," King said.

"Good," Evans said. "And make sure to go back to the vehicle and grab water as you need it. We don't want anyone getting dehydrated out here. My promise to your parents was to protect you and bring you home safe."

If that was true, King couldn't help but wonder, why were they on the run from Mundie instead of the other way around?

CHAPTER 22

King didn't want to make his curiosity about Blake's progress too obvious. He forced himself to sweep for twenty minutes with the metal detector, twenty minutes with not the faintest beep in his headphones.

Then, in case Evans or Moore was watching from the inside of the mobile home, he wiped his forehead as if he were really hot. Truth was, he did feel hot. But not sweaty. The arid wind took care of that.

He also noticed he wasn't feeling any of the panic-attack symptoms that always seemed to simmer just below his conscious thoughts over the past weeks.

It wasn't that he felt stress free. Just the opposite. His stress was as high as it had been since the Dead Man's Switch episode. So why didn't he feel the symptoms of panic? Maybe it was because his unease and stress had a legitimate cause.

He told himself it would be better to worry about that later. Right now, he needed to check up on Blake's progress. He walked to the Escalade, the black paint now filmed with dust from the wind.

He opened the liftgate and found a bottle of water in the cooler. He took it around to the side, tapped on the door, and slid in beside Blake.

Unbelievable how good the first gulps of water tasted.

"Got anything?" King asked Blake with a small gasp for air. He'd managed to drink half the bottle without pausing for breath. It also felt great to be in the cool air of the Escalade and out of the sun.

Blake said nothing. He made a few taps on the touchpad and turned the screen sideways for King to read. "It's a screen shot. I enlarged it to make it easier to read."

King saw an email filling most of the screen. He gave Blake a questioning glance.

"I hacked into Evans' email account," Blake said. "I can tell you the technical details later, but you'd think a CIA agent would be a little more careful with his password."

"Blake," King said, "I'm pretty sure hacking into a federal agency email account is also a federal offense. Federal and federal kind of go together."

"This from a guy who used a belt to choke-chain a federal agent this morning and shoved a sock in his mouth," Blake said. "Besides, I'd be more afraid of what's in the email. It's from two days ago, referring to a meeting yesterday morning."

King leaned closer and started reading.

To: evansc@ucia.gov

Subject: In-person meeting at Seattle office

"Evans C?" King said. "His first name starts with a C?"

"Charlie," Blake said. "Who knew?"

Now King did. He read the screen shot and the email.

Mr. Evans,

You have not been able to answer the questions to my satisfaction by telephone, and new information has come to my attention, so I have booked an immediate flight to Seattle. I will be in your office at 8:00 a.m. tomorrow to personally review the situation with you. Confirm your attendance by return email at your earliest convenience.

Don Mundie, Deputy IG

"IG?" King asked. "Don Mundie is IG. What's IG?"

"You're a fast reader," Blake replied. "Hang on. Let me show you another screen shot."

Blake swung the laptop his way, tapped the touchpad a few more times, and turned it back to King. "Same. Two days ago, referring to a meeting to take place in Seattle yesterday morning."

> **From:** evansc@ucia.gov
> **To:** mooreb@ucia.gov
> **Subject:** Meeting with IG
>
> Bill,
>
> I'm expected at a meeting with the IG first thing in the morning. I would assume that Mr. Mundie has alerted you to the meeting as a courtesy. Will you be in attendance? Also, when convenient, I would appreciate a chance to discuss this with you in person.
>
> Charlie

"Formal and uninformative email," King said.

Blake said, "I'm guessing Evans knows that all his CIA emails are subject to review at any time. Whatever is happening is not something he would put in email—or maybe only in a personal email account. I'd get a lot more complete picture if I knew his personal email address."

King wasn't listening too closely. He was rereading the email addresses.

"Um, hang on," King said. "Mooreb at a CIA email address? Didn't Evans tell us Moore worked security detail for the governor's office?"

"I thought it wouldn't take you long to catch that. I went through enough emails to tell you that beyond a doubt, Moore is Evans' supervisor. Whatever hunch led you to suspect something was wrong was a good hunch."

King was trying to absorb this. "IG?"

"It doesn't get prettier," Blake said. "Inspector general. As in 'Office of.' Mundie came in from DC on orders from the CIA Office of the Inspector General."

"That's the internal affairs investigator. Evans lied. They do have men to send into the field. Deputies. Like Don Mundie."

King groaned inside, thinking about the smelly sock he'd shoved into Mundie's mouth.

"Yeah," Blake said. "I've got one more email screen shot for you. From the day the meeting was supposed to take place. Yesterday."

King was numb as Blake grabbed the laptop again and pulled it up on the screen.

From: dmundie@ucia.gov
To: evansc@ucia.gov
Subject: Immediate suspension without pay

Mr. Evans,

Because you did not show up to our meeting as ordered by the IG, and because you are not responding to texts, calls, or emails, and because of the irregular use of CIA funds, you have been immediately suspended without pay. Furthermore, criminal charges have been sent to the federal prosecutor and a warrant issued for your arrest. My advice is to get legal representation and turn yourself in to your supervisor, Bill Moore.

Don Mundie, Deputy IG

King turned the computer back toward Blake.

"And here we are," Blake said. "Alone in the desert with a federal agent wanted for arrest and his supervisor, who is obviously in on it—two men who have misrepresented themselves to us."

Blake was the opposite of MJ. MJ was a drama king. MJ would be complaining about how he had to wet his pants again. Blake had once refused to talk even as someone held glowing cigarettes against his skin. By the tone of his voice, he could have been reading a stock-market report.

"Any suggestions?" King asked.

"Well," Blake said. "MJ is headed this way to grab some water, the keys are in the ignition, and the vehicle engine is already running. What's the first thing that comes to your mind?"

CHAPTER 23

Evans was also headed to the vehicle, about twenty yards behind MJ.

King had to make his decision quickly. He didn't have a driver's license, and because he lived on McNeil Island, he had not driven in traffic. On the other hand, Mack had shown him how to drive one of the prison vehicles, and the highway along the Yakima River had been almost deserted. If King could get down the gravel road to the highway, he could putter along at twenty or thirty miles an hour into the town of Yakima, ten or twenty miles downstream from where they were.

All that really mattered was getting away from the mobile home in the Escalade.

Unfortunately, the front end was pointed at the mobile home. King would have to back up and do a half turn to head down the gravel and back to the highway. And MJ was still ambling toward them, unaware of the decisions they were making inside the vehicle.

King knew he had to stay inside the vehicle. He scrambled from the middle row, squeezed between the front bucket seats, and tumbled into the driver's seat. He used the power button to lower the passenger-side window.

"MJ," King said. "Blake's got a question for you. Jump inside."

King said it as casually as he could, knowing that Evans was close enough behind to hear it.

MJ shrugged and kept ambling.

King gritted his teeth. He wanted to put the vehicle in reverse but worried that Evans would notice.

Finally, MJ swung inside.

As the door was shutting, King found reverse and gave it gas, half turning to look behind him as he drove.

"Hey!" MJ said.

"Got to go," King said. "Hang on."

He saw that Evans had begun to sprint. Not toward the vehicle, but to a point on the driveway ahead of them to cut them off.

And Evans won the race.

As King was putting it in drive, Evans reached the center of the road.

"Bulletproof windows," Blake said from the middle row. "Already googled it. You're good to go."

But Evans didn't draw his pistol. He simply crossed his arms and stood in the center of the gravel strip. Not enough room around him on either side to pass without hitting him.

King leaned into the horn and gunned it.

Evans responded with a sad smile.

King didn't make a calculated, intellectual decision. He went with his gut. The subconscious absorbs details and makes nearly instant decisions based on emotions. His nearly instant choice was based on Evans' sad smile and nonthreatening stance.

King swerved to take the vehicle off-road. The tires dropped into soft soil, and the undercarriage of the vehicle crashed onto the ridge of gravel at the side of the road. The vehicle wasn't going fast enough for its momentum to carry it off the ridge. Instead, the vehicle high-centered and lurched to a complete stop.

That's when Evans drew his pistol and walked toward them.

"We're bulletproof," Blake said. "Lock the doors. I can send an email out for help."

King hit the electric locks, making a click he was sure Evans could hear.

King cracked his window down.

"Stay where you are," King shouted. "Blake's about to call 911."

Evans advanced anyway, taking the last five steps to reach the vehicle. He reached out with his pistol and set it on the hood and then moved to the side, backing away from the vehicle.

"Don't know what's happening," Evans said. "But the pistol is yours. I'm going to back far enough away so that one of you can jump outside and grab it from the hood. That good enough to keep you from calling 911 until we talk this over?"

"King," MJ said. "Moore is headed this way too."

The noise of the vehicle must have drawn him out of the mobile home. Moore's hands were free.

"Bill!" Evans shouted. "We've got a situation here. Set your weapon on the front steps and proceed unarmed."

To King, Evans said, "Is that good enough to hold off on 911? You take my pistol, get back inside. Bill and I will stand here and have a discussion with you. We'll tell you the truth, and then you decide what to do."

"MJ?" King said quietly. "Blake? You guys make the decision. I'll trust you either way."

MJ said, "I'm a little late to this. I have no idea what's happening and why."

"We'll catch you up on it right away," Blake said. "Short of it, some emails make it look like Evans and Moore have been lying to us."

"But he gave us his pistol," MJ said. "Can it hurt to listen for a few minutes?"

"I hate guns," Blake said.

"Me too," King said. "I don't want it in the vehicle with us."

"Let's listen," MJ said.

"I agree." This from Blake.

King spoke to Evans. "We don't want the pistol, so leave it on the hood. And we're willing to listen."

"Thanks," Evans said. "You may have just saved a girl's life."

"Still listening," King said.

"I have a private YouTube account," Evans said. "I'll tell you how to sign in. There's a video you need to watch."

CHAPTER 24

With Evans and Moore sitting on the front porch, King turned his attention to the laptop that was perched between the bucket seats, giving him a view from behind the steering wheel and allowing MJ and Blake to lean in to watch.

Evans had only one video uploaded on his private account.

The hotspot connection was only moderately strong, and King kept glancing over at the front porch as he waited for the video to load.

"We're pretty sure she's underground," Moore called over from the porch as they waited for the video to come up. "That's why we're looking for tunnel entrances. And Murphy must have been here for a reason. To be close to her. That's our theory."

"Who is 'her'?" King asked.

As if on cue, a voice reached them from the screen. A female voice. Frightened.

"Hello? Hello?" the female voice said.

Looking into the screen, King saw a girl—high-school age—on a chair, wearing jeans and a loose Seattle Seahawks jersey. If she'd been a few years older, she could have been a cheerleader for the team. An off-screen light source shone directly on her face. Her hair was a messed-up blonde, and the light showed fresh tears on her face.

"Looks like a recording of a FaceTime conversation," Blake said. "You can't do it directly in FaceTime, but there are plenty of apps that make it possible."

"Hello?" she asked again. Her eyes widened in recognition as she leaned forward. "Paps?"

"Yes, it's me, Amanda. Are you hurt?"

King recognized the voice. Bill Moore. The cowboy-hat CIA supervisor who was pretending to be on security detail for the governor's office.

When the girl lifted her left hand to wipe some hair from her forehead, King saw that her wrist was in a manacle, and a chain from the manacle led off-camera. When her hand reached her forehead, the chain snapped tight.

King looked closer. The girl's ankles were bound with duct tape to the front legs of the chair.

"I'm not hurt, Paps. But he put me on this chair. There's an iPad in front of me on a stand. It's so good to see your face. I love you."

"Amanda..." The recording of Bill Moore's voice was low and urgent. "I'd step in front of a train for you. I'm going to do whatever needs to be done to get you back."

"He told me you have to follow his instructions," she said. Desperation was in her voice. She lifted both hands and showed how the chains to manacles on both wrists restricted her movement. "There's a hose. He..."

She sobbed for a few moments and then regained the strength to speak.

"I'm in a tunnel. He turned the hose on and let it fill this chamber to my neck," she said. "Then he drained the water. He says next time he'll let the chamber fill up to the top. That's why he let me take this call. To tell you that. And to tell you that he's tired of waiting for something from you. He says that starting right now, you only have seventy-two hours until he turns the water on again."

"Amanda, I love—" Bill Moore's anguished voice didn't have a chance to complete the sentence. The video came to a jarring end, and the screen went black.

CHAPTER 25

"We misled you," Moore said to King and Blake and MJ. He sighed. "No, we flat-out lied."

King and MJ and Blake sat in the mobile home, away from the heat and inside the air-conditioned space. The blinds were closed, which blocked enough light for King to pretend that the interior wasn't as ratty as the exterior.

Unfortunately, the near darkness didn't disguise the smell of stale cigarettes and body odor. How could anyone have endured living in this trailer?

They sat on kitchen chairs they had pulled into the living room area. King's mercifully brief first view of the interior—from the sunlight through the door as they entered—had shown a brown couch splotched with stains that gave it a giraffe-skin appearance. The carpet was littered with broken potato chips. Everything was old and grimy except for a magnificent flat-screen television, and even that showed dozens of greasy fingerprints.

"We had no choice but to hide," Evans said. "We can debate the morality of when to tell the truth and when to lie, but time is ticking on the seventy-two-hour deadline to save Moore's granddaughter."

"Granddaughter?" MJ asked. "Granddaughter?"

"I'm her paps," Moore said. "Her own father didn't return from the war in Afghanistan. I'm almost like her father. Delamarre knew I would do what it takes to get her back. She disappeared, and he got a message to me. Clear him of false terrorism charges, or she never returns."

Evans jumped in. "We *did* have to do this off the books. Delamarre made it clear that if Moore brought anyone into this on an official level, he'd never see Amanda again."

Moore nodded. "Only one person that I'd trust with my life in the organization. Evans. He lied about the governor's security detail, but he *did* tell the truth about our time together on a Navy SEAL team. I knew Evans would keep the operation entirely secret and whisper proof. He suggested bringing in you three to help us track Jack Murphy. Nobody would ever connect you to the CIA, and he said you could get the job done. Jack's the one we think is or was holding her."

Moore straightened in his chair. "And you guys *are* good. How did you figure out this wasn't what it appeared? What tipped you to try to run just now?"

King pointed at Blake, who was holding the laptop and all the cell phones.

Blake pointed at King, who wanted to hold his nose. The smell in the mobile home was like roadkill that had been in the sun for days.

Blake said, "King thought a few things were odd about your stories and asked me to do some quick searching. I wouldn't have been suspicious otherwise."

King said, "Blake hacked into Evans' department emails and—"

Moore's jaw went slack with surprise. "You hacked the CIA server?"

"Just Evans' account," Blake said. "His password wasn't that strong."

"Told you they were good," Evans said to Moore.

"We learned Don Mundie is a deputy inspector general. We found emails that you were both supposed to meet with him. And that when you didn't meet, he suspended Evans without pay and would file criminal charges."

"What I don't understand," Evans said, "is how he knew about you three. I thought I had covered all traces."

"Maybe the slush fund," Moore said. "Maybe the drone."

Evans rubbed his face and looked at King. "You didn't run me down in the middle of the road. Why not, after reading those emails?"

"You didn't bring up a weapon to stop me. I went on a hunch. If Mundie was right about you, first thing you would have done, I suppose, is pull out your pistol. The windows are bulletproof, but you couldn't know we knew that. From your point of view, a pistol should have been enough to make me slam on the brakes."

"It *is* from the governor's vehicle pool," Moore said. "I called in a huge favor on short notice when Evans told me to find a way to meet you guys on the highway."

"Just so I understand..." MJ said. "Moore, you are Evans' supervisor. Delamarre is trying to force you to clear him of false terrorism charges, so he arranged for your granddaughter Amanda to be kidnapped. You brought Evans in on this to find Murphy, who you think took her. Evans is using us off the books to help him. Mundie somehow found out about it. Now Mundie wants you and us. Is that about it?"

Moore nodded.

"How much time left on the deadline?" MJ asked.

"The FaceTime conversation took place about a day ago. As proof for me that she was still alive. We've already chewed up twenty-four hours."

"Forty-eight hours left then," MJ repeated. "We found Murphy, and they pulled him out of here without searching for Amanda because they have no idea that Amanda's been kidnapped and that she's the reason you've gone rogue, and if that leaks out, Delamarre promises to make sure you never see her again."

Moore nodded again.

"Then why are we sitting around?" MJ asked. "She could be in a tunnel anywhere within a hundred yards from here. I know you and Evans were taking this place apart to find anything that points to where she is. First thing we need to do is save her life, and once we do, you should be able to clear things with Mundie. Right? So Blake and King and I will head back out with the metal detectors."

Once again, MJ was a surprise to King, summing it up with such clarity. The guy liked playing clown, but that only led to people underestimating him. Which was probably why MJ played the clown.

"To be clear," Moore said, "you guys are with us? No questions, no doubts?"

MJ stood. "I want to start searching right now."

King stood, loving how determined MJ was.

Blake stood.

That's when the throb-throb of approaching helicopters reached them over the sound of the noisy air conditioner.

Moore jumped off his chair and peeked through the blinds.

A half-dozen patrol cars had pulled up, red and blue lights flashing.

"They've got us," Moore said.

Evans said, "Looks like Mundie delivered on his promise. We have nowhere to hide."

CHAPTER 26

A voice from a loudspeaker outside reached them. "You are surrounded by ground and by air. We have assault weapons. Moore and Evans, you know the procedure. Come out, hands on your heads. Then we'll deal with the three juveniles."

"This mobile home is a tin can," Evans said. "They won't use assault weapons to punch holes through it with King and Blake and MJ with us, but there's nothing we can do."

Moore spoke in a cold voice to Blake and King. "I trusted you when you said you hadn't called 911. I trusted you, and you sat there the whole time, knowing a team was moving in. When my granddaughter drowns, it's because of you."

"Trust us again," King said. "We didn't make the call. Blake, toss Evans your phones. Check the call logs."

Evans said, "Don't bother."

"Really," King said. The casual way Evans dismissed them stung King. "We didn't call 911."

"I mean don't bother—I *do* trust you." Evans gave a tight smile, understandable under the circumstances. "Somehow they tracked us here. But that doesn't matter. What does matter is how we get out of this now."

"Sir," Blake said. "Maybe it does matter knowing how they tracked us. We can use that information later."

"Later?" Moore said.

King understood and jumped in. "It's clear that you and Evans are going into custody no matter what. But if we three poor, innocent boys who didn't know what you dragged us into are able to go home, we'll still have more than twenty-four hours to try to find Amanda."

"Poor, innocent boys," MJ said. "Conned by cold, heartless—"

"They get it," King said, smiling.

"Don't forget lying," Evans said. "Cold, heartless, and lying CIA agents. I was the one who walked into the hotel room with Mundie on the floor and forced you three to remain silent while I pointed a gun at you and made you leave. Remember?"

"No," Blake said. "I don't want that to be part of the story. Kidnapping and a weapons charge against three juveniles? If this doesn't get straightened out, that would add another twenty years to your prison sentences."

"Much better if we play not so smart," MJ said. "You fooled us—that's the truth. And when I play not so smart, it's hard to tell if I'm acting."

Evans shook his head in admiration. He opened his mouth to say something, but the loudspeaker voice blared from outside.

"You have two minutes until tear gas. One minute and fifty-nine seconds. Fifty-eight. Fifty-seven..."

CHAPTER 27

"Fifty-six," the loudspeaker continued. "Fifty-five."

King found that the ticking clock added to his clarity. He loved the feeling of adrenaline. It was hard to believe that earlier in the day, he'd been fighting panic attacks in the safety of his mother's workshop.

An idea struck King.

King said to Moore. "From here, I can't tell that the remote that you're about to pick up is actually the television remote. It could be something to activate the explosives."

"Explosives?" Moore asked.

"How much extra trouble do you get into if you threaten that the mobile home is full of explosives and it turns out you were bluffing?" King said. "That way, you weren't really holding a gun to our head or anything. It would buy us some time to figure things out."

"Let me answer that like this," Moore said. He stood beside the door and opened it a crack, with the loudspeaker countdown reaching them clearly. "Forty-eight, forty-seven, forty-six..."

Moore yelled outside without exposing his face. "No tear gas! We've got the place rigged to explode if I let go of a timing device. You knock me out, and the whole place blows, taking all of you with us.

Same thing if you shut the power off. I blow everything up. So stop the countdown, and we'll negotiate."

The voice over the loudspeaker went quiet.

Moore shut the door and gave King a thumbs-up in the dim light.

Moore explained, "Lots of time they cut off the power so it's hot and uncomfortable, and the hostage holders just want to end it and get out."

"Perfectly played," King said. "Now, what do you want me to ask them when I get out there? What's going to help us the most when we look for Amanda?"

"I'm sending you out," Moore said. A statement. Not a question. But still a question.

"Sure. I tell them that you're holding a remote and that I couldn't see it well enough to guess what it was for. Then I bring you back some answers that can help us look for Amanda, and once you get the answers, you let all three of us out, and the two of you surrender."

"It's good," Evans said. "It's a good plan."

Blake said to Moore, "And while King's out there, taking his time getting those answers, I can jump on the Internet. With help from you and Evans, I can get to whatever files you think will help and upload them to an account on the cloud. We'll have ten, fifteen minutes for you to give me the most accurate inside information on Delamarre and Murphy. Also, I'll need access to some internal servers so I can set up a backdoor entrance to get in whenever I want."

"As in break national security measures and feed you classified passwords that would let you roam the CIA servers?" Moore asked.

"Pretend it's my birthday," Blake said. "And that you like me a lot. I'll be so happy."

Moore drew a deep breath.

Evans said. "It's a good plan. And they are all that we have."

Moore drew another deep breath. "They are all Amanda has. Three teenaged boys and less than twenty-four hours once they are clear to start looking again."

CHAPTER 28

The loudspeaker from outside blared again. This time, King recognized the voice. It belonged to Don Mundie. Given the short distance by air from Seattle to this side of the Cascades, Mundie must have arrived on one of the helicopters.

"Moore, you're a better man than that." Mundie's voice was calm and measured. "Let's not make things worse. You don't need blood on your hands."

"Ignore him," Moore said. "They've stopped the countdown, and we have a little bit of leverage on them. Let's use it to talk this out completely."

"I'm arguing that these three are Amanda's only chance," Evans said to Moore. "By the time they clear interrogation and get back to their parents, the deadline will be down to forty-eight hours. They'll have to sleep, and that means tomorrow morning it will be down to thirty-six hours. If we put them up at our three suites at the hotel and..."

Evans noticed King squint in an unspoken question.

"I prepaid for all three rooms for a week," Evans explained. "A suite for you guys, a suite for me, and a third suite five floors up under a different name as a hideout if we needed it. Budget didn't matter for us at this point. Good thing. If we can get your three families in there as a base, it will be better than isolating you on the island. That is, if Moore agrees to set you guys loose on this."

King nodded.

"I agree," Moore said to King, his tone showing that he was refocusing on the urgency of the situation. "First priority. You tell them you agreed to go outside and negotiate only if I sent emails to your parents letting them know about the situation. Tell them your parents are already on their way to the Seattle office. Make it clear that your parents have already responded to the emails. That way, Mundie can't put you in a holding cell and make you disappear for a couple of days."

"Better yet," Evans said, "let's go ahead and really send the emails to their parents. With instructions to have lawyers with them and waiting for the boys. We'll cover legal expenses later, I promise. All three families can camp out at the hotel suites tonight."

"Let's get on it," Moore said.

Moore turned to King. "When you give them the questions I want answered, they will tell you this is a national security situation and you are not cleared for the information. Tell them to email me the answers within the next fifteen minutes, and if the answers are suitable, we'll surrender and give up the remote."

"Yes, sir," King said. He gave Blake a glance. "Can you forward those emails to yourself without a trace so we have the answers ourselves?"

"Nope," Blake said. But in a blissful way. "But I can take photos of the screen with one of the other devices and upload the photos of the emails to a secret cloud account. When we're all finished, I'll delete everything, erase the phone, and put it on the oven burner. They'll have no way of knowing what we did. That should cover us."

"We'll put all our devices on the burners," Evans said. "That will destroy the devices, and the smoke will add credibility to the explosives threat. After we're gone, they won't come in here until the explosives experts give it a thumbs-up."

MJ said, "I'll turn on the stove so it's as hot as possible when we're ready to discard the devices."

All this should work, King thought. The CIA would send the three of them back to the Seattle hotel, believing that the teenagers had fallen for lies about a situation that didn't exist. Then for the three of them, the race against time would begin to stop the water from filling up the chamber.

"I'm ready," King said to Moore.

"Good," Moore said. "The first question you need to get answered before we surrender Blake and MJ is how Mundie managed to get the inside track on this."

Three minutes of coaching later, King opened the door slowly.

"I'm coming out!" King said. "My name is William Lyon Mackenzie King. My hands will be on my head. Please don't let Moore blow up the mobile home and my friends!"

King eased his way outside and saw Don Mundie behind a group of SWAT guys.

"And Mr. Mundie," King yelled, "I'm really sorry about the whole sock-in-the-mouth thing!"

CHAPTER 29

A few hours later, Mundie shut the door behind him, moved across the small room, and sat down at a polished table across from King, somewhere in the heights of the downtown building that housed the FBI. It was just the two of them, King in handcuffs.

Until then, King had been sitting alone for twenty minutes. The entire time he was acutely aware of a video camera near the ceiling, the black lens pointing at him.

"I've had a chance to talk to Michael Johnson and Blake Watt," Mundie said. "They've given me nearly everything I need to know. So all I want from you are a couple details to fill in the blanks."

"Sir," King said, "I need to go to the bathroom."

"Talk first."

"Badly."

"Talk first."

"Really badly," King said.

"Let's hear why Evans and Moore hired you," Mundie said. "And by the way, I'm okay if you wet your pants."

"The other kind of bathroom," King said. "Are you okay with that? I'm not enthusiastic about it for obvious reasons. When my lawyer gets here, he or she won't like it either. And my parents—"

"I don't think you understand," Mundie said, voice cold. "This is a national security situation, so it falls under the Homeland Security Act. You don't have the rights given under normal criminal charges. That means no lawyer, no parents. Especially because the email that Evans tried to send from the standoff situation never reached his lawyer. You're on your own here."

King didn't believe that. He thought Mundie was running a bluff. Evans had promised a lawyer, and King trusted Evans.

"I can keep you in a cell in this building for months and not even have to lay charges," Mundie said. "You have no rights because you belong to the government. You're considered a terrorist, and we make captured terrorists disappear from public view."

"My stomach hurts," King said.

"Deal with it. Let's begin with why Evans reached out to you and your friends."

"For our trip to Disney World?" King asked. "And how we met Snow White and the Seven Dwarfs?"

"Stop talking about Disney World," Mundie said. "It doesn't make me happy at all."

"I'll say," King said. "You don't look like Sleepy, Sneezy, or Bashful either."

King waited a pause. "But maybe Grumpy."

Mundie slammed the top of the table with the open palm of his right hand.

King managed not to giggle. Mundie's reaction was proof that MJ and Watt had not given Mundie everything that Mundie wanted to know.

All three of them had agreed ahead of time that no matter what, each would stick with a story about visiting Disney World and meeting Mickey Mouse, making up any details about the trip that they wanted. They were stalling for time because they believed Moore's promise that legal help would be on the way, despite Mundie's threats.

"Listen," Mundie said. "We are the good guys. Evans and Moore—they are the bad guys. You have chosen the wrong side, and it's going to ruin the rest of your life. Here's your chance to change sides. You talk for a few hours, we let you go, and your life continues as normal. All I need is as much information as you can give me about what the three of you were doing for Evans and Moore. You'll be saving your future, and you'll be doing a big favor for your country."

Mundie tilted his head as he rethought what he'd said. "Not a favor for your country. A duty for your country."

King felt the first tickles of doubt. What if Evans and Moore *were* the bad guys? He pushed away the doubt, thinking about the girl tied to the chair.

"Sir," King said, "can you explain to me exactly what's at stake here? How it impacts national security?"

"I wish I could," Mundie said, softening his tone as if he realized he had an opening with King. "But it's classified."

"You're asking me to make a decision, but you don't trust me enough to give me the information to make that decision?"

"Unfortunately," Mundie said, "that's how it needs to be."

"Unfortunately," King said, "I have to go to the bathroom."

Which was definitely true.

"We talk first."

"Well," King said. "The lines at Disney World were long. But there's an app that shows you the most efficient way to get in as many rides as possible."

"Are you kidding me here?" Mundie said.

"No, sir," King answered. "Are you iPhone or Android? It's an iPhone app for sure, but probably on Android too."

"I was referring," Mundie said, steel back in his voice, "to this whole Disney World shtick."

"If you didn't get enough details from Blake and MJ," King said, "I'll help."

Mundie stood. "I'll be back in about an hour. I'm not interested in being here when you mess your pants. *If* you're telling the truth about needing a bathroom break."

It wasn't something King wanted to think about, messing his pants.

He wondered if MJ was facing the same dilemma. Wow, would Mrs. Johnson have something to say about his underwear then. And talk about a rash.

As Mundie began to walk to the door, a knock came from the other side.

Mundie opened the door. King saw past Mundie. There were two men in suits—FBI or CIA—and a woman in a long navy-blue skirt and jacket, maybe midforties. She had blonde hair and held a briefcase.

"Sir," one of the men said. "This is Tanya Daniels."

"I'm an attorney," Tanya said crisply. She looked at King and spoke. "How are you doing?"

"Okay," King said. "But I need a bathroom break."

Tanya turned her gaze back to Mundie. "You'll uncuff him, of course."

"No. What I'll do is escort you to—"

"Please," she said. "The more you threaten me in front of your subordinates, the worse you'll look when you have to back away from those threats. My email from Moore is extremely detailed, and I've already instructed my secretary to release it to the media if he doesn't hear back from me in an hour. You know, in case you do something silly, like try to bludgeon me with the Homeland Security Act and lock me in a room somewhere for six months. It won't play well in the media, you know, that the CIA is detaining three young men who were hired by the CIA in the first place under false pretenses. And that—"

"Maybe you and I need a quiet conversation somewhere," Mundie said.

"Sure," she answered. "First, get this young man out of handcuffs. Second, escort him to a bathroom. And third, get him and his two friends something to eat."

"This is a matter of national security," Mundie said. "And—"

"And I'm getting tired of hearing that," she answered. "The parents of all three young men are in the lobby of the building right now, waiting to see their sons. Unless I make a call, in about twenty minutes, a television crew will be there to ask them how they feel about their sons being taken prisoner by a US government agent."

Mundie held up his hand to stop her from saying anything more. He turned his shoulders to speak directly to King.

"Hamburgers okay with you?"

"Yes, sir," King said. "And maybe a chocolate milk shake?"

CHAPTER 30

"When is it okay to lie?" King said to his parents.

King, Mack, and Ella overlooked the waters of the Seattle seafront from a fifteenth-floor suite of the luxury hotel. Blake and his parents were in suite 1010, where Blake and MJ had spent a couple days tracking down Jack Murphy for Evans. MJ and his parents were in the room Evans had been using.

It was ten p.m.—fourteen hours after Mundie had first picked up King by helicopter, eight hours after Mundie had taken Moore and Evans into custody at the mobile home, and two hours after Mundie had reluctantly given in to legal pressure and released King and Blake and MJ to their parents.

King was almost too exhausted to sleep. But tomorrow morning there would be less than twenty-four hours left before…

He tried to force that image out of his head but was unsuccessful. Of the water slowly rising and Amanda struggling to lift her chin as high as possible for as long as possible.

"It sounds like you're going to try to talk us into allowing the three of you to keep working for Evans and Moore," Mack said. "I know you guys could have lied and continued without our knowledge. Even though we're adamant that it's government business and you should not be put at risk, I'm very glad you didn't try to do it behind our backs. That would have very plainly been a deception that would have hurt our trust of you, because eventually, we would have found out."

That had been King's argument to Blake and MJ. That deceiving their parents would have hurt them and hurt their parents. A lot. They had expected, however, that by being open with their parents, eventually they would have been clear to continue.

That had been a heated discussion, an hour earlier, with all three sets of parents sitting in this suite. The division had been generational. King and Blake and MJ saw no danger and were honor bound to help Moore and Evans. Their parents were just as adamant that already the boys had been deceived into joining a CIA internal battle that put them on the wrong side of the law. If the Office of the Inspector General was involved, the IG and the entire CIA had the authority to resolve the matter. The boys had just been cleared of wrongdoing, and to get involved again would threaten their futures.

On the other side of the argument, King and Blake and MJ had promised Moore that they wouldn't reveal that Amanda was in danger. That put them in the same dilemma Moore had faced. Yes, revealing that a girl's life was at stake might justify what he and they had done and what they wanted to do. But according to the man holding her hostage, it would almost certainly guarantee Amanda's death once it was leaked. King and Blake and MJ had been able to tell their parents only that it was of utmost national security and that they couldn't reveal why.

"I'm not trying to start the argument again," King said. He doubted he'd be able to sleep tonight, worrying about Amanda held prisoner in a chair in a chamber somewhere, waiting for the water to be turned on again. He guessed that he knew what he and Blake and MJ would do next—disobey their parents.

Lying was something that could destroy a relationship. In a dilemma like this, King hoped, at least their parents could still respect them for believing in something strongly enough to accept the consequences for going ahead with the search anyway. It was a horrible choice, but King couldn't see a way around it. And he felt miserable for it.

King continued. "I am seriously looking for a serious discussion on this. That's a double serious, which shows how serious I am."

He was thinking about all the deceptions that had already occurred. Men he respected, including Evans and Moore, were in an organization built on secrecy and, by extension, deceit. Did that mean the CIA was morally wrong as an organization? And that all the American people were just as guilty because they supported the existence of the organization? King couldn't answer that.

On a personal level, Evans and Moore had lied to King and Blake and MJ about the reasons for looking for Murphy, and the three of them had understood the reasons for the deception after those reasons were revealed. So did that mean the ends justified the means? That it *was* okay to lie sometimes?

Mack could see that King was really searching and gave a nod of acknowledgment.

"I'm going to give you a famous question about lying," Mack said, "and then give you an answer I heard from a preacher. And then my response to that answer. Ready?"

CHAPTER 31

"Ready," King said to his father.

Ella sat on the couch, her legs tucked beneath her. She was sipping on tea and looked content to be an audience to the discussion.

"Here's the question," Mack said. "You have hidden some Jews in your house to save them from execution. Nazi guards knock on the door, asking if any Jews are in the house. Lying is wrong, but delivering them to be executed is also wrong. Do you choose a lesser wrong to save their lives?"

King opened his mouth to answer.

"Hang on," Mack said. "I didn't address that question to you. I'm giving you that question so you can hear the answer I heard from a preacher."

King shut his mouth to listen to Mack.

"The preacher said that the decision was made before you took in the Jews to hide them. That if you were brave enough to hide them, you'd better be brave enough to protect them. He said you should not lie, but you should open the door and tell the guards that it's a sin to take away Jews and that the guards should repent and pray for forgiveness. Then slam the door and accept the fact that you will probably become a martyr and that the Jews will die."

King opened his mouth again, but Mack waved him into silence.

"At that point in the sermon," Mack said, "my head nearly exploded. From my perspective, his answer was so illogical and goody-two-shoes that I was embarrassed. The point of hiding the Jews was to protect them. From my perspective, it would take just as much bravery to lie to the soldiers, realizing that if you were caught, you would be executed. It's one thing to sacrifice your own life, but to suggest that you should deliberately choose to let other people die just so you could deliver a mini sermon on sin and repentance to Nazi soldiers is…is…is…"

Mack sputtered with anger and then calmed himself. "What sometimes gets me about public Christianity is how it seems so judgmental and…"

He stopped, obviously realizing the issue was important to King. "Look, in the Bible, there's an Old Testament story about a woman named Rahab who lied to protect some men from Israel from being killed. And those men were spies, which means they too were practicing deception. Nowhere in the Bible does it say what she did was right or that she was sanctioned for it. But she *is* commended for the faith and obedience that followed in her later life. What I'm saying is that there is no easy answer and this needs a lot of discussion."

"So," King said, "life is messy and complicated and—"

He didn't have time to complete his statement. The hotel room phone rang.

Ella answered and listened, and then she laughed as she spoke into the phone mouthpiece.

"The president of the United States," she said. "Nice prank."

Then she frowned. "Sure. Three minutes."

Ella hung up the phone and shook her head. "Speaking of lies, Blake's mother insists it *is* the president. We're wanted in their room. Apparently it's important that we have a private FaceTime conversation with, yes, the president of the United States."

CHAPTER 32

"So," MJ whispered to King, "like Obama, this president of the United States is also black..."

King elbowed him to try to silence him.

"...and a woman?" MJ finished.

Looking into the FaceTime camera was an athletically built black woman a couple years younger than King's mother. The woman was wearing a dark pantsuit. Her hair was trimmed short, and her smile was neutral.

Blake had propped the iPad in front of the hotel flat-screen. The flat-screen was connected to a small Apple TV box. Blake was using the hotel's Wi-Fi to stream Airplay to the Apple TV so the image on the iPad played on the large flat-screen. The iPad camera caught most of the group. Three sets of parents, King, Blake, and MJ. MJ was in a pair of pajamas and didn't care that everyone else was still dressed as they had been during the day.

"My name is Kelli Isaac," the woman on the screen said in a crisp, no-nonsense professional voice. "Thank you all for agreeing to have this conversation. Before you meet him, as you probably know, the accepted way to address the president is as Mr. President."

"Yeah, right," Jim Watt mumbled. Blake's father was trim with thinning blond hair. "The president. This is a joke."

"I'm sorry," Kelli said from the television. "I couldn't quite hear that. Perhaps anyone who wants to speak should step forward from the group."

"It's all good," Mr. Watt said, raising his voice. Then lowered it. "If you like practical jokes."

Mrs. Watt elbowed him.

King could tell his own father was skeptical too. Mack's arms crossed his chest.

"You're undoubtedly wondering why the president would like to speak with you. But first I need a verbal agreement that what is discussed will not go beyond your three families, and I also need a verbal agreement that if you break the confidentiality, the CIA will prosecute you to the fullest extent of the law. I must stress, this *is* a matter of national security."

"Cow patties," MJ's father whispered. "That's what this is. Cow patties. Like we're really going to talk to the president."

"Is that a verbal agreement to both, Mr. Johnson?" Kelli asked from the screen.

"Um, yes," Mr. Johnson said. Then he glared at Blake and spoke from the side of his mouth. "How sensitive is that iPad microphone?"

Not much earlier, a courier had shown up to deliver the Apple TV box, cables, and a microphone.

"Mr. Johnson?" Kelli asked. "Further comments?"

"No," Mr. Johnson said and glared at Blake again.

Blake shrugged.

"Verbal agreements from the rest of you, please," Kelli said. "If you don't mind, do it one at a time, calling your name as you do so. For full disclosure, I am obligated to let you know that the conversation will be recorded. Let's begin with William King and then Michael Johnson."

King stepped forward, seeing himself in the small corner box of the television screen of the FaceTime conversation.

"My name is William Lyon Mackenzie King," King said. "And I agree to the conditions of this conversation."

He stepped back, and MJ went next. The seriousness of the situation was so heavy that MJ didn't clown around.

After MJ, each person did the same.

"Good," Kelli said. "The president is in the room with me, and I'm going to switch to the rear camera so he can address all of you. I will, however, be in this room at all times, and when your conversation with the president is finished, I will give you final instructions. Are we clear? If so, just nod."

King found himself nodding with the others.

"Excellent," Kelli said. "And here is the president of the United States."

She leaned in as she touched the screen to flip to the rear camera.

"Hello," said the president of the United States. "Thank you for taking the time to meet with me. Parents, I hope I can change your minds because I need the help of your three sons."

CHAPTER 33

"First," the president said, "I'd like to thank Blake and Michael and William for doing their best to assist agents Evans and Moore during the past few days."

It *was* the president's voice; it *was* the president's face. He was sitting in a chair in a spotlight that put the focus on him, blurring the background into vague darkness. He was wearing a casual shirt and dress pants.

King felt slightly dizzy. Even though Kelli Isaac had prepared them for this, it was still too unreal.

"Blake," the president said, "would you mind waving at me? I've been given photographs of each of you, so I know who you are. But since I can't shake your hand, I hope a wave in return will suffice."

Blake waved, standing proud and tall. The president waved and saluted him.

"Michael?" the president asked. "I see you are dressed for the occasion."

"I'm sorry about my president, Mr. Pajamas," MJ said. In his jitters, he barely managed a wave. The president smiled indulgently, probably accustomed to people getting nervous around him, and waved and saluted MJ.

"William?"

King waved and in return received the same dignified wave and salute.

"Parents," the president then said, "you should be proud of your sons. Despite what you might have heard from Deputy Inspector General Mundie, Evans and Moore are not rogue agents. They are working directly for me and were sworn to secrecy."

The president paused to let that sink in.

"Yes," the president said. "They are not even allowed to let the inspector general know of my presidential directive. Unfortunately, I'm not in a position to step in and get them released, or that will reveal something I'm in no position to reveal, which is the very reason that Evans and Moore will remain in lawful custody until this can be resolved."

He gave them a grave, presidential smile. "This puts me in a very difficult position. I need—and I stress, I really need—for the mission that I put into the hands of Evans and Moore to be successful. So parents, let me speak to you first. Blake and William and Michael are in the best position to continue. It's of utmost national security that they spend the next two or three days as a replacement team for Evans and Moore."

Mrs. Watt had raised her hand. The president nodded. "Yes. Charlene Watt, right?"

"Mr. President," she said, her voice quivering, "you'll understand that as parents, we are extremely concerned about the safety of our sons."

"Ms. Isaac has fully briefed me on the security logistics," the president answered. "We have a full team in the suite across the hallway from you. They have complete surveillance of the lobby, stairwells, and hallway."

Mr. Watt raised his hand.

"Yes, Jim," the president said.

"To me that kind of security detail suggests they are in danger. What kind of attack are you expecting?"

The president's smile was warm. "That's the same question I would ask about my children. I'm sorry to have alarmed you. We are expecting no danger. Your sons will be continuing the same kind of cyber investigation they began. However, my directive is that your sons are to be as safe as if they were my own children. I want to be as prepared as possible."

Mack raised his hand. This, it seemed, had become protocol for the conference.

"Mr. President, what kind of cyber investigation?" Mack asked.

"Mr. King," the president answered, "here is where I hope you can trust the word of the president. I am not at liberty to tell you. If you agree to let your sons assist me, they will be briefed by one of my representatives. They will be allowed the option to decline the operation, but either way—involved in the operation or refusing the operation—they will also be sworn to secrecy and not permitted to divulge anything of what they learn, not even to the six of you parents."

"I'm not sure if I like that," Mrs. Johnson said. "Oops."

Mrs. Johnson put up her hand and waited for permission to speak. "Mr. President, I'm not sure if I like that."

"I understand completely," the president answered. "I wouldn't either if I were you. Unfortunately, those are the conditions that must be in place." Then he smiled. "However, I think I can safely put a ten-year limitation on the binding oath of secrecy. When those ten years have passed, they can tell you what they did and why it was vital to national security."

From the flat-screen, the president surveyed all of them and said nothing more.

Mack put up his hand again, and when the president nodded, Mack asked, "Could the parents leave the room for a few minutes for a discussion?"

"Of course," the president answered. "My time is short, however. I hope you can appreciate that."

"I'm okay with it," Mr. Johnson blurted. He looked at his wife. "Right, honey? I'm okay with it?"

"Yes you are," she said.

"Um," Mack said, "this seems to me an all-or-nothing situation. If any of us aren't okay with this, I'd rather not have to point the finger at anyone for refusing the president's request. Much better to come back with a group decision."

"The Watts are okay with it," Mrs. Watt said. Beside her, Jim nodded.

Mack sighed. "Well then. Ella?"

Ella nodded.

"Then the King family is okay with it," Mack said.

"I am grateful," the president said. "Very grateful. My regret is that our fellow Americans will have no idea what they owe you. My representative will be dispatched immediately from DC and should arrive in Seattle within hours. Young men, will you be ready and alert by five a.m. for your briefing?"

"Yes, Mr. President," King and Blake said, accidentally in unison.

"I would always be ready for briefs that come from you, Mr. President." MJ colored as he realized how that could have be misinterpreted. "Not briefs, like, you know, briefs. But..."

MJ stalled out of embarrassment and said, "I am so sorry, Mr. President. My brain has hiccups sometimes."

"Please don't apologize," the president said with a laugh. "Getting called Mr. Pajamas was hilarious. My wife is going to like that story. Thank you again, and I hope to speak to you in a few days after a successful mission."

The camera switched back to Kelli Isaac.

"Thank you," she said. "You'll be seeing me at zero five hundred tomorrow. I'll be sleeping on the plane, and I suggest you get as much sleep as possible while I cross the country. Tomorrow is going to be a long day."

The screen faded to black.

"Who called the president Mr. Pajamas?" MJ asked with indignation. He looked at the parents and his friends. "Really—who would do that?"

CHAPTER 34

King was awake at three a.m. His parents were asleep in the bedroom that adjoined the hotel suite.

King wanted to sleep. He was exhausted. He'd tossed and turned but really hadn't found slumber.

His brain would not shut off. He couldn't shake the image of Amanda tied to the chair and a chamber that would be filled with water. To him, that reason to continue what Evans and Moore had been doing was far more compelling than a presidential request.

Although, wow. The president!

Hard to believe, but King seemed to have no choice but to believe. In a few hours, he expected, things would be clearer.

That was another reason he couldn't sleep. A combination of excitement, anticipation, curiosity, and worry.

For the hundredth time, King speculated on what the president needed that was so crucial and classified that Evans and Moore had to keep it from the rest of the CIA—and what all this had to do with Delamarre and Amanda.

As King began to turn over some questions in his mind for the hundred-and-first time, a new thought hit him.

Strange.

He turned the new thought over a few more times.

Really strange.

He reached out in the darkness and bumped his hands on the table a few times until he felt his smartphone.

He sent a text to MJ.

Let's meet in the lobby. Now.

It didn't take long for a response. His phone vibrated in silent mode.

Sure.

You didn't ask me for the code phrase, King texted back. The night before, all three families had agreed to use a code phrase to identify each other in cyberspace or through any other messages.

The return text from MJ's phone was short. *You woke me up to test me on using the code phrase?*

King was even shorter. *No. But still need it.*

MJ responded. *Who do we work for?*

As King read the code phrase, he could hear MJ sighing.

King sent him back the answer to prove nobody else but King was using the phone. *We work for Mr. Pajamas.*

King smiled in the dark. Nobody was going to let MJ forget his first words to the president of the United States.

Yes we do, MJ replied. *I'll go to the lobby.*

King slipped into his clothes. Using the light from his phone to see in the darkness of the room, he scribbled a note on a piece of hotel stationery and placed it on his pillow in case his parents woke up and wandered into the suite.

I'm in the lobby with MJ to talk about working for Mr. Pajamas. Call or text if you need me.

Although King was tired, he was glad to be doing something. Because for Moore's granddaughter Amanda, the clock was ticking.

CHAPTER 35

King chose the lobby so his conversation with MJ wouldn't wake up his parents.

They sat on a couch across from the front desk. It seemed safe. Hidden speakers played soft, classical musical. The clerk had seen them come and go a few times and gave them a tired wave. King was glad the clerk was there as a witness to prevent anyone—if anyone was so inclined—from forcing them to leave the hotel.

"Did I wake you up?" King asked.

"You kidding?" MJ said. "I feel like I've had fifty cans of cola. I don't know if I'll ever sleep. Think about it. POTUS!"

"Potus?"

"Did you put that in all caps in your mind as you said it?"

"Huh?" King said. MJ's thoughts were often difficult to follow.

"Capital 'P', capital 'O', capital—"

"I get that part," King said. "POTUS?"

"Exactly. Those of us close to him use that term. President Of The United States."

"Ahh," King said. "And others just call him Mr. Pajamas. Happy to see his briefs."

Finally, that silenced MJ enough for King to begin where he'd wanted to start.

"I don't know if I entirely trust what happened," King said, kinking his neck first one way and then another. The pullout bed of the couch in the suite had not been too comfortable.

"We went through that with all our parents," MJ said. "It would be impossible to fake the president's part of the conversation."

"Not disputing that," King said.

Immediately after the FaceTime conversation, Mr. Watt had wondered if what they had seen had been based on some kind of special effects, like in movies. They had decided that in movies, the digital actors were scripted. But in their FaceTime conversation, the president had responded to questions and to movement. No one could have anticipated what MJ would have been wearing, and yet the president noted MJ's pajamas and said, "I see you are dressed for the occasion." Only an actual person on the other end of the FaceTime conversation could have seen MJ in those pajamas. And only an actual person could have seen each one raise his or her hand and then address that person by name.

"What's bothering me," King said, "is that the president called you Michael, and he called me William. If he was working with Evans, he would have called me King and you MJ. Like when Don Mundie pretended he was picking me up for Evans and didn't call me King."

"Maybe the president was being formal," MJ said.

"Yeah, that's a possibility. That's why I didn't say anything in front of our parents during the group conversation."

"So you called me down to the lobby to bring up something that doesn't even worry you?"

King snorted. "No. But add those doubts to something else..."

MJ was rocking back and forth where he sat, hyped with energy. "Talk to me, Kinger," MJ said, as if this were part of a movie and MJ a cool intelligence agent.

King let that slide and said, "Look, we all watched the replay of the conversation two or three times, right?"

MJ nodded. "That's one of the reasons we agreed it had to be the president."

Blake's iPad was jailbroken, and he had dozens of apps that weren't available at iTunes, including an app that recorded FaceTime conversations.

"What's the first thing the president said to us?" King asked.

"I need the help of your three sons," MJ said. "The president!"

"No, that's not what he said," King closed his eyes and did his best to hear it again in his mind. "Thanks for taking the time to meet with me. Parents, I hope I can change your minds because I need the help of your sons."

"The help of your *three* sons. Three. You missed the word 'three.'"

"MJ," King said, trying not to show his frustration. "What about the entire sentence you missed. '*Parents, I hope I can change your minds.*'"

"Need to get the 'three' part right, wouldn't you say?"

"Of course," King said, reminding himself the fastest way to end an argument with MJ was to agree. "I should have remembered."

"Okay then." MJ nodded in satisfaction. "Knew it. Absolutely knew it."

"Here's what's really bothering me," King said. "How did the president know our parents had decided not to let us stay involved?"

MJ wasn't stupid, King thought, as he watched his friend's eyes widen in understanding.

"How did the president know we had come clean with our parents and told them that Evans and Moore wanted us to help?" MJ said in an excited voice of comprehension. "And how did he know our parents had said no way would they give us permission? That conversation happened only a couple hours earlier. In the hotel room. A private conversation."

"Yeah," King said. "Think about the time line. Our parents tell us no. We eat in our hotel rooms because we called for room service. A courier knocks on Blake's door and delivers an Apple TV box and cables and says to expect a FaceTime call."

"It would be like someone else had been in the room, hearing our parents tell us no."

"Or?" King asked.

"Face-palm," MJ said. "Or someone had the room bugged. Room 1010. Where MJ and I had already been a couple of days."

King nodded.

"How about we send Blake a text to see if he's awake," MJ said. "Whatever is happening, we need to figure it out before the five o'clock briefing."

King looked at the lobby clock. Three thirty-five.

That gave them less than an hour and a half.

CHAPTER 36

King and MJ stood in the lobby until the headlights of a taxi swung into the drive of the hotel, and then they hit the cool, early morning air. It would be a couple hours before the sun brightened the sky.

They opened the rear doors of the taxi, one on each side, and swung themselves inside. The seats were plastic and sticky, and the interior smelled like cigarette smoke.

MJ jabbed his fingers at a No Smoking sign on the window.

"Like I can't see you back there?" the cabdriver said. He was nearly bald, with fringes of hair over his ears that looked like wisps of straw. "I smoke when I don't have passengers. Get over it or get another cab."

With time ticking, they weren't going to wait for another cab. This one had taken ten minutes.

"We're over it," King said. "We need to get to a Walmart. Bellevue's the nearest one."

"Bellevue?" the driver said. "That's going to be at least forty bucks. Good thing traffic is light this time of night, or it might cost you sixty. I'll be wanting that money before I drive you out there."

King found some bills in his pocket. There was a protective plate of Plexiglas between the passenger seat and the front seat. King pushed forty dollars in fives and tens through a small slot.

The driver made a big deal out of counting it twice. He folded it and tucked it into the front pocket of his shirt.

Still, the driver left the cab parked.

"We're in a bit of a hurry," King said.

"Yeah, well it's forty bucks each way."

"And I'll be happy to pay it when we get back to the hotel," King said. "We're going to need you to wait while we do a bit of shopping."

"I'm happy to wait here until I get another forty bucks."

"MJ," King said, "can you use the flashlight on your phone and get the number on that No Smoking sign?"

"Whatever," the driver grumbled. He threw the cab into gear and headed down the quiet streets of downtown Seattle.

One hour remained before the arrival of the president's representative. And about twenty-four hours before a tunnel chamber was flooded with water.

CHAPTER 37

Because of the situation, something was comforting to King about the familiarity of the interior of the Walmart—the bright fluorescent lights, the long line of carts, the checkout stands, and the endless aisles that were empty at this hour.

It was too early for a greeter in a light-blue vest to be waiting for them. Ahead, a janitor was riding a floor-polishing machine, leaving a light sheen of water on the tiles.

"Electronics section," MJ said. "This shouldn't take long. Blake said he went online and confirmed they have the radio in stock."

King heard the whoosh of the automatic door open and close behind him. He saw a woman in blue jeans and a hooded sweatshirt with the Oregon Ducks logo on it. She had short brown hair and no makeup.

Her eyes swept over them, and she grabbed a cart and pulled it loose with the usual clanging. The carts always seemed to stick together.

Something bothered King about what he'd seen, but MJ was pulling on his arm.

"Time's wasting," MJ said. "The cab driver is charging us a buck a minute to wait."

King didn't care about the money. It came from a slush fund and it wasn't his. He wasn't going to waste it, but he was going to do what was necessary to save as much time as possible. Even arguing with the cabdriver over the fare would have taken a precious minute or two.

King followed MJ. He wanted them to run, but that would draw attention. Nobody ran in a Walmart unless it was to chase a two-year-old who escaped from a cart.

Still, they managed a fast pace. They reached the electronics at the back of the store. The flat-screen televisions were dark. King couldn't help but wonder what time the manager decided it was worthwhile to turn them back on again.

The store had a hush to it, something King liked. It felt peaceful. Even though he didn't like the process of shopping, he wished that a girl wasn't about to die and that he could just amble up and down the aisles.

As MJ squatted in front of a shelf full of portable radios, King saw the woman again.

Her cart was half full with assorted items.

That was fast, King thought with admiration. He and Mack avoided shopping with Ella partly because she was so deliberate and picky about her purchases. She'd look at every shirt in the men's department, going back and forth until she found exactly what she felt Mack should wear.

That was *fast*, King thought again. Not only how quickly the woman had put stuff in the cart, but how she'd managed to cover the distance from the front of the store to the electronics department.

As King glanced over again, the woman had her eyes on some candles. She grabbed a couple and threw them in the cart.

And then King realized what had bothered him at the front of the store.

No purse.

He realized full well that it was a stereotype to assume that all women carried purses. He also realized it was a stereotype to assume that all women shopped as carefully as Ella did.

On one hand, it did make sense that a woman who preferred the efficiency of carrying a driver's license and credit card and some cash in her pocket would be likely to shop as if she were in a race. On the other hand, how many women who wore jeans as tight as this woman did would put stuff in their pocket if they were conscious about curves?

Then again, maybe she didn't care about fashion. And maybe King was overthinking things.

Any other time, King would have been prepared to dismiss his overactive imagination. But this wasn't any other time. It was too logical that the CIA would have wanted to keep an eye on the situation. After all, the hotel had plenty of surveillance cameras, and it wouldn't have been too difficult to assign a couple of agents for a night.

King just wished he would have thought of that earlier instead of now. He and MJ had just waltzed out of the hotel and into a cab that was easy to follow. And no doubt Mundie would want to know why King and MJ were in a Walmart at this early time of the morning.

King walked to another aisle and began loading up on DVDs. He didn't care what movies he picked—he just wanted the woman to see them shopping for movies.

"Cool," MJ said, behind him. "Good idea. Make the government pay for that. But really, *Mary Poppins*?"

King ignored MJ. "We need duct tape. But first, cookies."

Anything to make it look like the radio wasn't the most important thing. King also wanted to see if the woman would follow them.

Which she did—far enough behind that she didn't appear to be tailing them. But a coincidence, King thought, should only go so far.

"Make sure you get chocolate chip," King said in a light tone. King wasn't about to say, "Don't look now, but we're being followed." Because if he did, MJ would be sure to gawk, and they'd lose the element of surprise.

If the woman was one of Mundie's team.

One way to find out. See if she showed up in other departments. Then King would be 100 percent certain it wasn't a coincidence.

Which she did. So it wasn't.

CHAPTER 38

"Here's what I want," King said, stopping near the basketballs. "Bounce this a few times, will you?"

"I think you're losing it, bud," MJ said. "We were supposed to be in and out. I'll give you the movies and cookies because that only took a minute, and hey, it's movies and cookies. But buying a couple of dresses and wigs? And why did you send me for duct tape?"

That had been inspiration on King's part. He figured if the woman was on Mundie's team, that meant King and MJ had been tailed from the hotel. It meant that probably at least one other person was back at the hotel waiting for them.

If so, King also figured she was calling in what their purchases were. A couple of dresses and wigs would make it look like they intended to disguise themselves. So if someone was back at the hotel, they'd be looking for a couple of ugly and badly dressed girls.

King's goal was to confuse Mundie's team as much as possible. He wanted to ride back to the hotel without them knowing it, and that meant finding a way for the woman to be stopped here. He wanted them guessing what was going on. The dresses would add uncertainty.

So would the purchase of a couple of fishing rods. He'd leave the dresses and wigs and fishing rods in the cab but keep the radio.

So the next step was to make sure the woman didn't leave Walmart when they did.

King tucked the DVDs under his arm, scooped up a basketball, and tossed it to MJ.

MJ dropped the bags of cookies and his roll of duct tape to catch the ball. He missed, and the ball bounced passed him.

"Not cool," MJ said. He leaned over to pick up the cookies and duct tape. "Like, this is making me mad."

"I'll explain when we get outside," King said. "We need to go."

He was thinking his distraction probably worked. The woman was an aisle down, but she'd been watching them.

At the checkout, King looked behind him.

He saw exactly what he'd expected.

The woman had left the cart in the aisle and was taking only a few items to another sales clerk. If she checked through all the items, King and MJ would be long gone.

The clerk in front of them was a redheaded guy with a full beard, equally blazing as the hair on his head. He wore wire-rim glasses and had a relaxed attitude.

"Gentlemen," he said. He smiled at the cookies and movies. "Sometimes you just need some cheap entertainment, right?"

Then he frowned. "*Mary Poppins*?"

"Yeah," King said. "My friend here can't get enough of Julie Andrews."

"Hah, hah," MJ said.

King paid for the radio and the cookies and the movies and grabbed the bag. He said to MJ, "How about I meet you at the cab. Want to take these?"

"Need the bathroom?" MJ said.

"I'll explain in about a minute, when I get there."

MJ shrugged and headed out the door. King saw the woman watch MJ and then glance back at him.

Then King leaned forward. He spoke in a soft voice to the clerk. "I'm scared."

"Huh? *Mary Poppins*? Now *Jaws*, that's scary."

King said. "No. See that woman at the other till?"

"Yeah," the clerk said.

"And see that cart with all the stuff in it in the aisle?"

"Yeah."

"She loaded up the cart but isn't buying anything."

The clerk sighed. "Somebody's going to have to put it away. Nothing I can do about it."

"But that's why I'm scared," King said. He realized he was about to tell a lie. But a girl's life depended on them. That made it right, didn't it? "See, I heard her talking on her cell to a friend. She said she had a gun."

"What?" the clerk said. "Gun!"

"Think about it," King said. "You pretend to load a bunch of stuff, and then when it looks good, you break away for the till."

King pulled out a whistle that he'd taken from the sporting-goods section. He hoped the woman hadn't seen him do it when MJ was dropping the cookies. He didn't want her to have any warning.

"I didn't know what to do," King said. "I've called the cops, and they're on the way. But I thought if we used this, we could get security here and clear the store."

"I'll call security," the clerk said, reaching for a phone by the till. "It won't take them long."

He spoke urgently into the phone and then hung up.

"Good idea," King said. He'd taken the whistle, thinking he might need it as a distraction in case the clerk didn't buy into his story. "How about I go talk to her. I'll ask for directions or something, and that'll give security a chance to get her before she leaves the store."

King tossed the whistle to the clerk. "Don't use this unless you absolutely need it."

"I want to run," the clerk said. "A gun?"

That was King's bet. If she was on Mundie's team, she'd have a concealed weapon.

"Look," King said, "I'll pretend I need to ask for directions. That should keep her from pulling the gun. She'll want as few witnesses as possible."

It was bad logic. There were cameras all over the store. A person who was really intending to rob the Walmart at this hour would know that. But all King needed was to have the woman detained. If she was part of Mundie's team, she wasn't a danger to him. Before the clerk could answer, King walked toward the woman.

"Hello," King said as he got close. "Did Mundie send you alone? Or is someone waiting outside?"

She gave King a look like he was an idiot.

"Mundie?" she said. For a moment, King felt doubt. But it was a little late for that. He could see security guards headed their way. One male and one female.

"Don Mundie," King repeated. "Your boss's boss."

"Don't go weirdo on me," she said.

King's doubts grew. Had he just made a horrible mistake? If she wasn't following them and it was just coincidence...

Definitely too late. From behind, security guards on each side grabbed her arms.

"What are you doing?" she half shouted as she tried to whirl.

"She's the one," King said. The loose hoodie was the perfect place to hide it. If she didn't have a gun, the guards would detain her anyway. And King was ready to bolt.

The female guard didn't hesitate. She began by patting the woman's back, just above her jeans. The logical place to tuck a pistol.

The widening of the eyes of the female guard was enough for King to know that she'd found something. And the woman tried to twist away. That made it certain.

"She's armed," the female guard said. "Armed!"

That's when the redheaded clerk began to blow the whistle in loud, panicked blasts.

"Gun!" the clerk shouted. "Gun! Clear the store!"

King stepped back.

Good luck, he thought. *Good luck trying to pull a badge to clear up the confusion.*

He joined the first shoppers who were scurrying out the door. It was great to see MJ waiting beside the cab, munching on cookies.

"All right," King said when he got there. "We're good to go. And now would be a good time."

That just left them to find a way to sneak back into the hotel.

CHAPTER 39

Back in the cab, King sent a text to Blake.

Are you able to put the hotel cameras back on a loop?

Almost immediately came a reply.

As easy as netting fish in a barrel.

King clicked the virtual keyboard on his own device. *Good. Check your email.*

King had changed plans. He wasn't going to leave the fishing rods and dresses and wigs in the cab. Instead, he and MJ were going to direct the cab driver to drop them off a few blocks away, ditch the stuff they didn't need, and hurry with the radio back to the hotel.

It looked like they had time. Just barely.

As the cab left the parking lot of the Walmart, King heard sirens.

A half a mile down the road, the red and blue of flashing lights were easily visible in the darkness. Three cars were racing toward them.

The cabdriver slowed to let the cops go past them. King turned his head to follow the progress of the flashing lights. Seconds later, brake lights went red. The cops were slowing to go into the Walmart parking lot.

MJ was watching too. He bit into another cookie. "Hah. That's a Walmart that doesn't mess around with shoplifters."

If the cabdriver hadn't been up front and able to hear every word, King would have told MJ about what had happened. That would come later. For now, King needed to send an email to Blake.

> Here's why we need the loop on the hotel video cameras. I just found out that Mundie's team is still tracking us and probably knows we're still in the game. Someone is probably sitting in front of monitors. Loop all the hallways where we have rooms. Also, loop the cameras in the back stairwell in the northeast corner. Then, when I send you a text, go to the ground level and let us in through the exit door.

King showed the screen of his device to MJ and let his friend read it. He was ready to squeeze MJs leg hard if MJ started to blurt out any questions.

MJ said nothing—just nodded.

King hit Send.

Perfect. Maybe. With the woman on Mundie's team back at the Walmart, Mundie wouldn't know for sure where the cab was headed. He'd have to do a lot of head scratching to figure out why King and MJ had purchased a radio and a couple of dresses and wigs.

In the meantime, they'd be in the hotel room, waiting for whoever the president sent. And anyone monitoring the hallway would not see the knock on the door at five a.m.

If the knock came.

But it had to come. A girl's life depended on it.

CHAPTER 40

Thirty-five minutes remained before the five a.m. arrival of someone sent by the president. Blake looked at the lobby clock and grinned. "We still have ten minutes to spare."

King understood. Blake had tiptoed into his parents' bedroom and reset the alarm clock from 4:15 to 4:40 a.m. The three of them wanted to be back in room 1010 without the need to answer questions from the Watts about why they'd stepped out for a while. If the room did have recording bugs in it, they didn't want the conversation overheard by whoever had planted the bugs.

Now, however, it would be perfect when Blake's parents woke and started talking to the three of them because the conversation would be a natural follow-up to the night before, and Blake would need that conversation to try to detect the presence of the recording bugs.

"One second," Blake said. He took a few steps to the desk.

Already, the lobby was starting to become active with businessmen down early to catch the free coffee at the breakfast bar.

"Excuse me," Blake said to the woman behind the desk. There had been a shift change. The guy who'd been there when King and MJ were on the lobby couch just after three a.m. was already gone.

"Yes?" the woman said. Pleasant.

"I'm on the tenth floor," Blake said. "I can't seem to log on to the network."

"That's strange," she said. "You don't need a password."

"It's 'hotelwifi'?" Blake asked. "All one word, lowercase?"

"Not ours," she said. "Ours actually has our hotel name. You're getting that one too, right?"

"Well," Blake replied, "that explains it. Thanks."

As King and MJ followed Blake toward the elevator, Blake said, "Yes. That does explain it."

"Explain what?" MJ asked.

"In the cab, I did some more googling," Blake said. "One of the articles explained that recording devices sometimes use a Wi-Fi network to transmit and forward the data."

"We don't need the radio then?" MJ asked. "That could have saved me—"

"You'll get the money back," King said. "We've got the receipts."

MJ was stingy. But that meant he was the one of the three who most often had available cash. Because he didn't spend it.

Blake said, "It will be good to have confirmation. Because that will make us feel better about moving on to stage two of our little plan."

The elevator chimed, and the door opened. Two businessmen, each in a suit and each with rolling luggage, stepped out.

King and MJ and Blake stepped in, and MJ hit the button for the tenth floor.

"Let's get it done," King said. "Twenty-four hours and counting before some homicidal maniac starts filling that chamber with water."

CHAPTER 41

There was a knock on the door of room 1010 at precisely five a.m.

Mack checked the spy hole in the door and looked back at the assembled group and nodded. He opened the door, and the athletically built black woman with trimmed short hair from the FaceTime conversation stepped inside the room.

She gave everybody her now-familiar neutral smile. She had used it at the beginning of the FaceTime conversation to introduce the president and again at the end to announce she was on the way.

Now, however, she was wearing a cashmere sweater and blue jeans.

"Good to see you, parents," she said. All three families were in room 1010. "I expect you'll be in the other rooms, and you can call anytime to check up on us. In the meantime, I can assure you that local security teams have moved into place. So we are good then."

She opened the door, pointed the parents out, and said, "Every minute matters. I'm glad you understand."

Mack made the first move, and the other parents followed.

When the suite had cleared except for Kelli, King, MJ, and Blake, she gave them a smile that was warmer than her professional one.

"I need coffee," she said. "I need it bad. Surely in a place this fancy, we should be able to brew something."

* * *

With coffee in hand, Kelli sat on a chair facing the three, who were on the couch in the center of the suite.

"I was serious when I said we have no time to waste," she said. "So I'm going to start by talking about the Harry Potter movies. I don't want to know if you've watched them. I only want to point out that the movies made something famous that until recently seemed impossible for the real world—invisibility cloaks."

She sipped from the coffee and sighed with satisfaction. "Imagine the difference in warfare and intelligence work if agents, soldiers, tanks, or even airplanes could be rendered invisible."

Blake was unable to help himself. "I know—it's mind-blowing! Composite films with nanoscale patterns stacked in a three-D architecture! That kind of structural manipulation allows precise control over the propagation of light. And with electromagnetic resonances over the three-D space—"

"Stop, stop, stop," Kelli said. "You're hurting my head. But I'm impressed. You not only knew about what's been publicly released on invisibility materials, but you even know the science behind it?"

"I knew it too," MJ said.

"Yeah," King said. "MJ absolutely knew it."

"I need more coffee," Kelli said, smiling. "Hard to keep up with you guys."

She took a large sip and then continued. "So if you're up to speed on that, now I'm going to move into classified material. It's one thing to build a fabric, it's..."

She stopped. Blake had put up his hand.

"Yes, Blake?"

"So far," Blake said, "as I understand it, this material has only been manufactured at micron-scale sizes. Are you saying the technology is there to make it cloak-sized?"

"Probably within months. And not only cloak-sized, but tank- and airplane-sized. But that's not enough. The cloaks, or sheets, also need software programming."

Kelli stood and grabbed one of the cushions MJ had tossed on the floor to make room on the couch. With her right hand, she held it in front of her at waist height. "For this to be invisible, you would need to see what's behind it."

She moved her left hand directly behind the cushion. "If you didn't see my lower arm and wrist and hand, that would be a visual cue that something was abnormal. If the cushion just disappeared but there was a cushion-sized area of darkness, the cloak would not be effective. Agreed?"

"Sure," King said.

"If you had a camera on the cloak at the back of the cushion, the camera could show the image of my hand and project that on the front. But you would need a wide-angle camera, and even then, the image would be strange enough to again cue your eyes that something was abnormal."

Kelli looked at Blake. "So how do you solve that?"

"Some kind of film with thousands of little eyes," he said. "Transmitting the shifting images behind the cushion."

"Sharp," she said. "I can see why Evans and Moore wanted to work with you guys."

King jumped in before MJ could speak. "MJ absolutely knew that too."

"Yeah," MJ said, either unaware or pretending to be unaware that King was giving him a verbal jab.

"The trouble is," Kelli said, "the computing power to make it happen takes monstrous amounts of memory to embed it in the fabric. And that's where Delamarre's software comes into play. His research team found a way to make it happen."

She paused. "Are you aware of his reputation?"

"He's on the run for terrorism links," MJ said.

"Aside from that. His reputation for secrecy as the head of a software company."

"He's like Steve Jobs was," Blake said. "Like with the first iPhone. Jobs made sure each research division was working on just one piece of a puzzle. No one team knew exactly what they were building."

"Yes," Kelli said. "Now imagine all the pieces are completed, and Jobs is the only one who has all of them together. And then Jobs steals all of it from the company. Even though many of the pieces have been duplicated and stored on the cloud, it takes all of them to deliver the product. So if several key pieces are missing…well, you get the picture."

"Yes," King said.

"So the situation is this," Kelli said. "Delamarre began the software research for the invisibility cloak for the government, but when it came together, he decided it had so much value, he wanted to put it on the open market. In return, the government threatened to arrest him for terrorism and ruin not only his reputation but the whole company's reputation as well. After Apple and Microsoft, his company is—was—one of the biggest. Delamarre thought the government was bluffing and proceeded without them. As you know from the headlines, the government wasn't bluffing. He was indicted for terrorism and escaped custody. Now he needs them to publicly admit that the charges of terrorism were based on faulty intelligence, but the government won't do it unless he hands over the key pieces of software."

"Got it," MJ said.

King and Blake nodded.

"So Delamarre's plan was to force someone in the CIA to find files that prove the terrorism charges were put in place to blackmail him to give up information."

"Moore," King said. "With Evans."

"But it goes way deeper than that," Kelli said. "There are betrayals of national security that do involve terrorists, and they're hidden deep inside the CIA. That's why the president is involved. And that's why I'm here to get your help on his behalf."

"We're ready and willing and able," MJ said. "Anything for POTUS. You and me, on his team."

She gave MJ a funny look, then reconsidered anything she'd been about to say.

"Yes," she said. "Anything for POTUS."

"What do you need?" Blake asked.

"You have information from Moore on how to hack into the CIA main servers," she said, "so let's start there and see where it leads us."

CHAPTER 42

This time, King decided he didn't need to use his belt like a choke chain. He hated the thought of attacking a woman, and besides, he and MJ and Blake had already planned their next move.

"I have this thing about not touching a monitor screen with my fingers," Blake told Kelli. "Drives me crazy to see the poke mark. So follow the arrow of my mouse and look at this. It's okay, you can lean over my shoulder."

MJ was in the way. This had been planned.

Blake said. "Dude, give her some room. It's important that she sees this. We're in the email server. There's some serious stuff here."

MJ stepped aside.

"Okay if I look over your shoulder while you're looking over his shoulder?" MJ asked Kelli.

She nodded, hardly giving him any attention.

MJ stood behind her. He reached behind his back, and King was ready—pillowcase in one hand, duct tape in the other.

King put the pillowcase in MJs fingers.

In one swift move, just as they had practiced with Blake, MJ dropped the pillowcase over Kelli's head like a hood.

"Hey—" she started to say, raising her hands to pull at the pillowcase.

King was ready. He tossed the duct tape from Walmart on the desk for Blake. King grabbed her left hand. MJ left the pillowcase over her head and grabbed her right hand.

She tried to kick and lost her balance.

"Let...go..." she grunted.

King was glad she wasn't screaming. But he'd guessed that she wouldn't. If she screamed for help, she'd have to explain what she was doing in the room—something she didn't want to do.

King and MJ held their grips, holding her wrists.

She landed on her knees with her hands above her head.

King pushed her left hand to center, and MJ did the same with her right hand.

"You...guys...are..." She didn't have a chance to finish.

Blake had the duct tape and made a quick wrap around her head, guessing where her mouth was. He guessed correctly. There was a muffled high-pitched noise, as if she was trying to yell at them through a closed mouth.

"Hurry," King said to Blake. "She's strong."

Blake moved to Kelli's forearms, and with three more wraps, they were pinned together. But when they let go, she stood and kicked blindly.

"Ankles!" King said. Duct tape was so much better than the shoelaces they'd been forced to use against Mundie. Was that only the day before?

"Don't want to hurt you," King said to Kelli. "Don't fight this, okay? It's going to happen anyway, so make it easy on yourself."

She kicked again.

"Oh man," King said. "I hate this."

He judged the next kick and then grabbed her ankle. She stood like a stork on her other leg, unable to swing that leg.

King pushed her backward, toward the couch. She had to hop to keep her balance, and he pushed her in baby one-hop steps until the back of her knees hit the couch and she fell backward into a sitting position.

She kicked with her free leg.

"Guys," King said. "Some help here?"

MJ grabbed Kelli's other ankle. She was so strong that King and MJ each had to lock her ankles under their arms and hold them against their ribs.

Blake darted in and wrapped the duct tape around her knees. Another few rolls around her calves. And then, when King and MJ dropped her ankles, he wrapped them securely together.

They backed away.

The pillowcase hid her face. Her arms were in front of her, her hands resting.

More muffled sounds from below the duct tape around the pillowcase.

"Scissors?" MJ asked.

King nodded and then spoke to Kelli. "We don't want to hurt you. We're going to cut away the pillowcase above your mouth so you can breathe okay and see. But I'm going to be using scissors, so don't move. If you're good with that, raise your hands."

She waited a moment and then slumped her shoulders and raised her hands.

MJ appeared with tiny scissors from the toiletry kit in the bathroom.

King snipped away the pillowcase and pulled it from her head.

The bottom half of the pillowcase was still in place, with duct tape around it and her mouth.

Their eyes met. She was glaring with laser anger. King was glad her hands were not free.

"I know," he said. "This isn't what you expected. But now we need some answers."

She shook her head violently from side to side. Negative.

"I thought that might happen," King said. "Time to bring in the big guns."

Her eyes widened.

"Our parents," King said. "They're going to find it very interesting that our room was bugged. And since you're not CIA, they're going to be as curious as we are about who sent you and what you expected to get from us."

CHAPTER 43

King had been at Seattle's FBI building on Third Avenue twice before. The first had been during the Dead Man's Switch episode—the FBI had put him into contact with the CIA, and that's where he'd met Evans. The second time was yesterday, when Mundie had questioned him and Tanya Daniels had freed him. The CIA had used the FBI offices for meetings following the arrests of Evans and Moore.

The building, with concrete gray ribs and reflective windows, stood across from a Starbucks. King knew what to expect going inside and didn't hesitate, walking across polished granite tiles to the receptionist.

"Hello," he said. "I was here yesterday with Don Mundie, who is a deputy inspector general for the CIA. It's urgent that I speak with him again."

"Sir," the receptionist said with a scornful curl of her lip, "this is the Federal Bureau of Investigation."

She had been chewing on a fingernail as he approached. He glanced at her nails. Chipped nail polish. She was in her midtwenties and smelled slightly of body odor. King's judgment was that the woman wasn't particularly motivated to make decisions outside of her job description.

"Yes," he said, knowing that if he stopped being polite, he had no chance of getting through to her. "I know it's FBI. But the CIA doesn't have a Seattle office, so CIA agents have used the offices here before. I know that because I was here yesterday. It's urgent that I speak with Don Mundie."

"I suppose I could call someone who could call a supervisor, but it may take a while."

"It's very urgent," King said. He thought about his conversation with Mack. *Should a person lie to save a life?*

King went with the truth. "I can't tell you the details because if I do, the girl involved will be killed. But I need to speak to Don Mundie."

"Oh my," the receptionist said in bored voice. The scornful curl came back to her lip. "Such pressing matters. You should try something original, like a conspiracy about UFOs hidden at Roswell."

King fought his frustration. He said, "Bomb."

"What!" The scornful curl snapped into a straight line of lips pressed in anger. "I know you're joking," she said. "But that kind of threat can get you put in jail. And the paperwork for me is crazy. So don't go there, okay?"

"You mean for a bomb threat you have no choice but to press some kind of button?"

"Please," she said. "Don't go there."

"Can you get the supervisor here immediately? Otherwise..."

"So," she said, scornful again. "Let me get this straight. You're threatening to bomb-threat me?"

"Bomb," King said, tired of messing around. "There's a bomb in this building and it's going to go off in less than ten minutes. I know because I'm the one who planted it."

He caught a slight movement of her hands under the counter. He guessed she was pushing an alarm button.

Within seconds, he was surrounded by agents with assault rifles.

"Thanks," he said to the receptionist. "That's all I needed."

CHAPTER 44

Don Mundie glared at King across a conference-room table on the seventh floor of the FBI building. King had been waiting only a few minutes, standing by the window and watching people in the plaza across the street wandering in and out of the Starbucks.

"I don't care how many lawyers you have," Don said with gritted teeth. "A bomb threat at a federal building—that's a minimum five years in a penitentiary."

"I don't think that's the issue here," King said.

"Then tell me the issue," Mundie said. "Now that it's just you and me. Instead of you and me and Mommy and Daddy and the lawyers that Mommy and Daddy bring with them."

"The issue is that one of our hotel rooms was bugged. I don't think it was you who bugged the room. So that leads to the question of why Moore and Evans would do it."

"You have a great imagination, son."

"No," King said, "just a friend who is nearly a genius. The bugs operate on an analog basis."

"You found them then?"

"No, we heard them. We swept the room with a Sony AM/FM radio."

Mundie squinted.

"The radio had a jack for earbuds. As we were talking, Blake tuned the radio up and down the spectrum. The bugs transmitted our voices to the radio. Because he was wearing his earbuds, whoever bugged the room didn't know we'd found them."

Mundie squinted again. "You can find bugs like that?"

"You have to understand the difference between analog and digital." King remembered Blake's explanation. "Digital sends out data in packets. It's all or nothing. Analog sends it out in waves. It can be crackly or clear, but you can adjust for that with volume. So, yes—"

"What I meant is that a cheap radio can do a bug sweep? When I think of the budget money we use for—"

"Sir," King said, "I'm not here to inform you that the room was bugged. Now that I've established that fact, I'm asking who would bug the room. And who learned last night that our parents told MJ and Blake and me that we couldn't work for Evans and Moore."

"Exactly. That was part of the agreement with the legal team you brought in here yesterday. That if there was so much as a hint of any future involvement—"

"Sir," King said, conscious of time slipping away, "our parents told us that last night in room 1010. They made it loud and clear that we were to drop everything. So loud and clear that it was loudly and clearly transmitted through the listening bugs in the room."

"I still don't see an issue here."

"Because about an hour after that, we were contacted by the president of the United States, asking our parents to reconsider."

Mundie laughed. "This is getting better and better. You know, I was mad when I was called from the airport to come back to this office. Now I've got a good story to tell my friends in Washington. That some schmuck kid thought he could get me to believe the president asked him to get involved in a CIA operation behind the back of the inspector general."

Mundie stopped laughing. "Okay, it's not funny anymore. Because this means you think I'm so stupid I'd believe you."

"There's a reason I asked for a room with a computer hooked up to a television screen," King said. "I'd like you to watch a private YouTube video."

Mundie glanced at his watch. "I have five minutes. After that, I'm on my way back to the airport. And the only reason I'm not going to press charges for your little bomb-threat stunt is that I don't want the paperwork. And I don't want to have to come back to Seattle."

King went to the computer, and when he clicked the keyboard, the screen at the front of the conference room brightened.

He jumped on the computer's Internet browser, found YouTube, and put in his account settings to get to the video Blake had uploaded.

The video opened with the president of the United States staring from the screen at Don Mundie and saying the words, "Hello. Thank you for taking the time to meet with me. Parents, I hope I can change your minds because I need the help of your three sons."

King hit pause because he heard the sound of a falling chair. He looked over to see Mundie on his feet, hands on the table, chair on the floor behind him.

Mundie was staring at the screen as if he'd just witnessed the start of World War Three. His mouth opened and closed a few times as he struggled to speak.

"Yup," King said. "The president of the United States. Or as MJ and Blake and I like to call him, POTUS."

"Keep it frozen there," Mundie said when he found his voice. "I've got to cancel my flight."

CHAPTER 45

Mundie surprised King with his next move because Mundie moved past King to a pad of paper at the end of the table and wrote, *This room is probably bugged too. SOP.*

"I'm canceling my flight," Mundie said, "because you've gone too far. It's one thing to make a bomb threat at a federal building, but to fake a video that impersonates the president of the United States—that I can't ignore. I've brought in a pair of zip-tie handcuffs just in case, and now it looks like I'm going to have to use them. I'm going to cuff you and take you to your parents. Got it?"

Mundie winked at King.

This was a threshold moment. Was Mundie pretending to pretend, just to get cuffs on King? Or was Mundie taking King seriously?

Mundie must have caught and understood King's hesitation.

Trust me, Mundie scrawled on the note. *This is seriously a national security situation, and I need your help without the FBI knowing it.*

With all the lies, King thought, how does a person decide what's true?

He decided Mundie's initial reaction—the chair falling, the hands on the desk, the jaws moving silently—was real.

King held out his hands.

Mundie slid out plastic zip-tie handcuffs from a pocket. Then he grabbed the entire pad of paper and put it in the inner pocket of his suit coat.

And King became Mundie's prisoner, paraded out of the FBI building in front of grim-faced agents who couldn't quite manage to conceal their glee that a teenage boy was being punished for trying to play big-boy games in the wrong sandbox.

*

Inside Mundie's rental car, Mundie dug out a pocketknife and cut the zip-tie handcuffs.

"Good thing about my clearance level," Mundie grunted, "is that I can have a pocketknife when I fly. Now let's find a place to talk."

Mundie drove them to a park near a public library.

He pulled the car over, stepped out, threw money into a meter, and hurried King to a bench in the shade of a tree. Hopeful pigeons hopped toward them, but Mundie scattered them with a wave of his hands.

"We record any meetings with representatives of other agencies," Mundie said. "I have to assume the Feebs would do the same to me. Cooperation only goes so far."

Mundie let out a breath. "Talk."

"About the video? I can show it to you from my iPhone."

"Don't need to see the rest immediately. I want your impressions of it."

"The president said he had asked Evans and Moore to assist him with something so secret that no one else in the CIA could know about it. Like there were bad agents, and Evans and Moore had to root them out."

"Okay," Mundie said. "You believed it?"

"Yes. At the time."

"You made the assumption that I might be one of the bad agents?"

"Yes."

"Yet you came to the FBI building to reach me and allowed me to cuff you."

"Yes."

"You have a reason for it?"

"Yes."

"Ready to give me more than a one-word answer?"

King nodded. "First, MJ and Blake and I agreed that it was strange that the president didn't call us by the names that Evans did. He called us William and Michael instead of King and MJ. But the bigger question was how the president could know he needed to change our parents' minds. That led us to discovering the bugs."

"You've covered this already."

"So who was bugging us and feeding the information to the president? If it was someone from the good faction of the CIA, then the good faction was already involved, and he could use them instead of us because the good faction would have known about Evans and Moore. But the president told us that no one else knew about Evans and Moore, so it couldn't have been the good faction."

"Good faction, bad faction. How about bad fiction?"

"Let me get where I was going," King said, "and you'll see I agree there's no good faction or bad faction. Because it couldn't be the good faction, and if a bad faction was bugging our room, why would they report to the president and try to get us involved after learning our parents didn't want us involved? So that meant someone outside of the agency had planted the bugs. Someone who wanted us to keep looking for what Evans and Moore were looking for."

"Now we're getting somewhere. It's Moore and Evans who went rogue, and they refuse to tell us why."

"With all due respect," King said, "I'm also going to refuse to tell you why."

"We were just starting to build some kind of relationship here," Mundie said, clearly irritated. "Don't pull this garbage on me."

"If I were you," King said, "I would assume that if Evans and Moore are prepared to risk jail time by refusing to speak, and that if I'm prepared to face the same thing, then it must be pretty important. So it might not be smart to shut me down at this point without looking for the person who put the bugs in the room."

"That doesn't put me in a better mood," Mundie said.

"And if I show you a photo of the person who bugged the room?"

That startled Mundie. "You were searched at the FBI building. You didn't have a photo."

"Not on me. But in the cloud. Lend me your smartphone, and I can pull it up for you."

Mundie unlocked his phone with a password and handed it to King.

King handed it back. "Can you download the Dropbox app?"

Mundie sighed. "I hate Dropbox. Too secure for us to crack."

It took Mundie less than a minute. "Here."

King entered his account info, found the photo of Kelli Isaac, and pulled it up on the screen. He handed it back to Mundie, expecting an aha reaction.

Instead, Mundie's eyebrows furrowed.

"Nothing," Mundie said. "This does nothing for me."

King hid the disappointment he felt. He'd believed that the photo would give him some good levers to pull with Mundie.

"And the president calling us on FaceTime? Shouldn't that be worth looking into?"

Mundie was silent for a moment and then gave his own one-word answer. "Yes."

"Then email this photo to someone in DC," King said. "See if that brings up any flags. You've come this far with me."

"Five minutes," Mundie said. "Five minutes more."

He walked away from the bench. King watched and waited and watched and waited. Finally Mundie returned.

"I'll drop you off at your parents," Mundie said. "This photo means nothing to the CIA."

"You mean drop me off so you can start your search for her without me? You think I'm so stupid I'd believe you and the pretended lack of interest in a video with the president?"

Mundie couldn't help but smile. "I can neither confirm nor deny."

"If you want her," King said, "I can get her for you. And a lot more. But only if in return you give me what I want."

CHAPTER 46

Forty minutes later, Mundie led King, in zip-tie handcuffs again, past the wide-eyed receptionist in the FBI building. King's internal clock told them they were down to less that eighteen hours before Amanda drowned.

Mundie had one hand on King's back to guide him. In his other hand, Mundie held a cloth bag with a drawstring.

A silent, square-jawed FBI agent—thanks to Mundie's earlier description, King now couldn't help but think of the man as a Feeb—escorted them to the elevator and, once inside, used a key to access the fifth-floor button.

When the elevator stopped and the door opened, Mundie said to the Feeb, "We'll take it from here. All I need is the magnetic swipe."

"Not a chance," the Feeb answered. "SOP makes that impossible."

"This is not a standard operation," Mundie snapped. "My direct boss reports directly to the president on a weekly and sometimes daily basis. Your direct boss is a lot lower down the food chain. Don't make me flex my muscles here, or you'll be spending a couple years in an office in the middle of Kansas."

They traded stares until the Feeb blinked first.

"Watch your back," the Feeb said, gritting his teeth as he handed Mundie a plastic card that looked like an ordinary hotel room key. "Any chance I get, I'll do my best to see you get to Kansas first. It makes me almost hope the prisoners you're taking out of custody manage to bust free and leave you hanging at the end of a noose."

Mundie stepped out of the elevator with King, and the Feeb stayed behind. When the doors slid shut, Mundie said, "See what I told you about agency infighting?"

"Yes, sir. I just don't understand why your diplomatic approach failed to create extra goodwill."

It took Mundie just the slightest of pauses to understand that King had been sarcastic, and that earned King a chuckle from the agent.

They walked down the hallway. King was aware of the video cameras in place.

"What's 'SOP'?" King asked, remembering that Mundie had also written the abbreviation on a note in the conference room earlier.

"Standard operating procedure," Mundie said. "And that's something you forced me to abandon about when you made a bomb threat to the Feebs. Because of it, I'm much crankier than I appear. Everything I do this morning will be reviewed exhaustively, and I'm thinking there's an even chance I'll be in Kansas soon enough to give that Feeb the last laugh."

Mundie stopped at an interrogation room and used the plastic card to unlock the door.

Two men inside looked at him from behind a table, both in orange jumpsuits.

Evans and Moore.

"King?" Evans said.

"Gentlemen," Mundie said, "it's your lucky day."

Mundie tossed the bag with a drawstring onto the floor. "You'll find your street clothes in here. Your friend here found a way to bust you loose."

CHAPTER 47

"Finally," Evans said. "A chance to talk to Murphy. Two floors down. Same kind of room."

"Would have been a lot easier if we had reached him first," Moore said. "Don't like it that we needed help to get there. Without King, we're still in orange suits. So, King, thanks."

"Just returning the favor," King said to Evans and Moore. "Thanks for setting us up with that lawyer and getting us out of there. She was a force of nature."

They were walking down a hallway on the ninth floor of the building. Both Evans and Moore were adjusting their ties. Their clothes were rumpled, but King doubted either would complain. Better than orange jumpsuits.

King didn't have a tie to adjust, but he rubbed his wrists, glad the pressure from the plastic zip locks was gone.

"She?" Evans asked. "She?"

"Tanya Daniels," King answered.

Both men stopped.

"I say something wrong?" King asked.

"In the mobile home, when we promised you legal help," Evans said, "I sent an email to my personal attorney. Clint Bortsky."

"Wasn't him," King said. "Really."

Evans pointed at an open office and the desk with a phone.

"Hang on," he said.

Evans slipped inside, leaving the door open. King heard the conversation clearly. He wasn't surprised when Evans came back to the hallway and said, "My email never reached him. He had no idea what was going on."

Moore said, "Someone showed up and got you loose?"

King nodded.

"That means," Moore said, "someone knew you were in custody and where."

King had to agree with the conclusion.

"Not CIA," Evans said. "Not us."

"Your parents?" Moore asked King. "Anywhere along the way, did you have a chance to call your parents before Mundie brought you here?"

"No, sir," King said. "Mundie kept telling us we had no rights and he would not call anyone on our behalf until we told him everything."

King saw a question appearing on Moore's face. "But all we told Mundie was the Disney World story. Like we agreed in the mobile home during the standoff."

"A third party sent the lawyer then," Evans said. "Someone who wanted you back in motion."

King nodded. "There's something you should know about a woman named Kelli who showed up at our hotel room this morning."

So he told them.

CHAPTER 48

King had seen Jack Murphy only on video footage taken from a drone that was moments away from being blown out of the sky by a SWAT-team missile. Then, Murphy had been in handcuffs, stumbling between two men as they dragged him away from the mobile home on the high desert on the other side of the Cascades.

Now, King sat across from Murphy in an interrogation room on the fifth floor of the FBI building.

King was flanked by Evans on his left, Moore on his right. Three against one. Mundie was in the hallway. A confidential interrogation of Murphy had been part of King's negotiation.

Murphy, still in orange, was Hollywood handsome—for the role of the guy who drank a lot during the day and had been doing so for at least a decade. Murphy was about the age of King's dad, but Murphy had deeper wrinkles and jowls and a trace of a beard that was showing lots of gray. His dark, curled hair hung over his forehead and showed lots of grease.

Even though his wrists were in chains and snapped to a ring on the table, Murphy's attitude was not defeat, but defiance.

He glared at Moore. "I should have known my ex-father-in-law was behind this. I miss a few alimony payments, and you bring in the Homeland Security Act. I want to thank you for the favor. By the time I finish suing the government, I'll be living in a gated golf community, and you'll be in a mobile home in the desert."

Murphy had been Moore's son-in-law? As King tried to absorb this new information, Moore leaned forward.

"What you don't understand about the Homeland Security Act," Moore said to Murphy in cold anger, "is that we can keep you in here for years, and you won't even get close to a lawyer. We can move you out of the country and make you disappear. The sooner you understand this, the better for you. Because I'm going to ask you some questions and—"

"All this for late alimony payments? I've always known you hated me, but talk about abuse of power!"

Moore said, "Mr. Evans here will list the charges you're facing."

Evans nodded, grim faced. Evans and Moore had rehearsed how the interrogation would go.

Evans said, "Kidnapping. Blackmail. Death threats. And about a dozen major charges for attempting to harm national security with illegal coercion to gain access to classified files. Want more? We can come up with more."

Moore jumped in. "All of it goes away if you tell us where Amanda is."

"Huh?" Murphy said. His defiance was replaced by genuine surprise.

"Amanda Moore. Your stepdaughter. My granddaughter. The one who chose her mother's maiden name instead of your name."

"Let me get this straight," Murphy said. "The whole SWAT-team thing and a day of cooling my heels in isolation is so I will tell you where Amanda is?"

"One-time offer. Take it now, or you won't be out of a federal prison until you're so old you'll need a walker to enjoy the freedom."

Murphy's expression became calculating. "Just so we're straight here. I tell you where Amanda is, and all charges are dropped. I go free."

"All charges except the kidnapping. That's going to get you ten years—seven with good behavior."

Murphy said, "And if the kidnapping charge is bogus?"

"Who did you give her to?" Moore said. "Where is she?"

"To her mother," Murphy said. "They're on vacation."

Moore launched himself across the table, and his right hand became a claw on Murphy's neck. Murphy had no chance to defend himself and gargled helplessly for air.

Evans pulled Moore away.

"Steady," Evans said. "Kill him and we won't get anything."

Murphy made circles with his chin, trying to stretch his neck.

"You're a crazy man," Murphy hissed at Moore. "Crazy."

"I'm going to go crazier," Moore said, "if I don't get answers from you. If you don't have her, you might have thought handing Amanda over to someone else would be an easy hundred grand, but now she's less than twenty-four hours away from her execution."

"What are you talking about?"

"Did you actually believe she wouldn't come to harm when you handed her off?"

"I didn't kidnap Amanda, which means I didn't hand her off," Murphy said. "I want to hear that part again about a hundred grand. What are you talking about?"

"You're an idiot," Moore said. "You actually thought if you opened four bank accounts and put twenty-five thousand in each, I wouldn't realize someone had paid you to kidnap her from her mother?"

"You're saying I have a hundred thousand in four different bank accounts?" Murphy started laughing. "Seriously?"

Murphy shook his chains, still laughing. "Come on then. Let me loose. I've got some money to spend."

Murphy stopped abruptly, seeing the look that Moore was giving him.

"Dude," Murphy said, "I have no idea what's going on. But I can tell you this. A few days ago, when I talked to your daughter, she said she was going on vacation with Amanda and that she wouldn't be back for a while. So let's get all of this settled and let me at the money."

CHAPTER 49

In the hallway, Moore said to Mundie, "Think Murphy was telling the truth?"

They'd shut the door on Murphy to join Mundie. Evans and King stood to the side. Evans winked at King as if King were in on the joke.

But King wasn't. All he knew was that the big hand on the clock had slid another sixty minutes closer to the deadline before Amanda's promised drowning.

"I think he was astounded by what he learned, which means he had nothing to do with the kidnapping," Mundie replied. "Someone snatched her and knew he'd be your first suspect. It was obviously worth a hundred thousand to that person to put the money in his account and confirm your suspicions. Do we know of anyone with that kind of money?"

"Delamarre," Evans said.

King looked back and forth. His face probably showed he was shocked. Shocked that Mundie had broken his word about letting them have a confidential discussion with Murphy, and shocked that Evans and Moore weren't showing any anger.

"Wouldn't do any good to pretend I didn't hear the entire conversation, would it," Mundie told King.

"Not when he's got as much on the line at this point as we do," Moore said to King. "Naturally, he'd listen in."

Moore looked at Mundie. "Just assure me it won't get into the hands of the Feebs."

"As much as I can," Mundie said. "It *is* their building. Ears could be anywhere and everywhere."

"Let's take it outside then," Moore said. "Starbucks is across the street. I'll buy."

*

The four of them found a round table beneath an umbrella. King normally didn't drink coffee—he didn't like the taste. But he'd ordered an espresso, triple shots, just to keep the exhaustion at bay. He hadn't slept much the night before.

Just as King was thinking that professional lying was second nature to these guys, Mundie began the conversation.

"Until you spent five minutes in that one cell waiting for King and me to arrive," Mundie said to Moore, "you and Evans had been in separate holding cells since we arrested you. And you were under observation for the short time the two of you were waiting. I can't see any way that you were able to collude ahead of time with each other or with Murphy to run your conversation with him the way you did. For that matter, I can't see any way you even expected King to negotiate you out of your cells to have a chance to talk to him."

"Thought those would be your conclusions," Moore said.

Mundie said, "So I accept that your time with Murphy was a legitimate interrogation. Furthermore, you admit you anticipated this and expected I'd listen in. That means your secondary purpose in there was to convince me you had a good reason to recruit Evans and begin an off-the-books investigation of Murphy."

"Successful?" Moore asked.

"In convincing me, yes. From the conversation, I understand your granddaughter has been kidnapped and you're under pressure to find her. The agency will take a dim view of your actions, but I understand it on a personal level. Still, I can't ensure there will be no disciplinary action—not yet. If we can get to Delamarre, the agency will probably be much more lenient."

Mundie let that hang there a moment and then said, "Here's where I'm at. King gave me a photograph of a woman who is posing as a CIA agent on behalf of the president. I'll let him explain."

"I need to ask some questions first," King said.

"We don't answer questions," Mundie said. "We ask them."

Then Mundie grinned. "Sorry. That's a reflex response. Standard operating procedure. What do you want to ask?"

"Jack Murphy," King said, directing his question to Evans. "You told me he was supposed to testify that Delamarre was a terrorist, and that's why you were trying to find him, right?"

Evans said, "I think I know what you're going to ask. Was that a lie? To you and your friends? The answer is yes. I needed to give you guys a reason to believe I had to do this off the books. Moore and I are so desperate to find Amanda...it was just one more deception."

King had his internal questions. When is it justified to lie? When is it okay to do bad things to stop bad people? He didn't know if he would be able to answer that in his own mind, but he knew the men in front of him practiced deception every day. For the United States. Was that morally okay?

Instead, he asked Mundie something that had been bothering him. "How long did you know it was off-the-books?"

Mundie directed a long and level stare at King. "Son, you barely have clearance to know what I take in my coffee. No chance am I going to tell you anything about our internal checks and balances, except to let you know that it's sophisticated enough to tell us something was happening within seventy-two hours of Moore accessing some slush funds."

Mundie shifted his stare to Moore. "And when this is over, there will be consequences."

Moore said, "If we find Amanda, I don't care if I spend the rest of my life in a federal prison. So maybe let's focus on what's in front of us right now. And start with listening to King talk about the woman who pretended to be CIA."

Moore and Evans turned total focus on King. When King finished, both looked thoughtful.

"No idea who she might be," Moore said. "Except that Delamarre wants the files that will clear him. Enough to kidnap Amanda and use that as leverage to force me to give him the files. He must have sent her."

"And he must have had the bugs set up in room 1010," Evans said. "It never occurred to me that he'd know we were there."

Evans gave Mundie a questioning glance.

"I have no idea either," Mundie said. "All I was told was that my biggest priority out here had been shifted. Find and apprehend the woman and put the routine IG investigation about you guys on hold. I received no information on why, and when I asked, I was told I didn't have the clearance. And I'm *in* the IG, so that should give you an idea of how hush-hush this is. I'm asking you guys, since all our cards are out on the table—do either of you know what Delamarre's original involvement was with the CIA? I can promise you it's not the invisibility cloak Kelli Isaac told King about. That's old stuff. Not everything about our research is on the Internet, but plenty."

"Beyond my clearance level too," Moore said. "I had no chance of finding the files that Delamarre wants, nor did I intend to look for them. My goal all along was to get my granddaughter back with the off-the-books special op with Evans. And without turning over any files to Delamarre."

Evans said, "Even if we get the woman, or Delamarre, chances are we'll never find out what the secret software is that you are keeping from us."

Evans glanced at King. "It's how we work. Need-to-know basis."

"Beginning to understand that," King said.

"And right now," Mundie said to King, "we need to know what you promised you'd tell me when you got Evans and Moore released. So where is the fake CIA agent you took captive?"

CHAPTER 50

King sat on the couch of the fifteenth-floor hotel room suite, dazed at the silence.

In that silence, the eyes of Moore, Evans, and Mundie felt heavy upon him.

He'd walked through it twice in disbelief. Housekeeping had cleaned the room and put fresh towels and linens in place. His parents' clothes were still in the bedroom.

Empty.

That was impossible. When he'd departed the room to go to the FBI building, King had put a "Do not disturb" sign on the door to keep the maids from checking the room, and Kelli Isaac had been bound hand and foot with duct tape.

And when he'd departed, Mack and Mr. Johnson and Mr. Watt had grimly promised that there was no chance Kelli Isaac would be allowed to leave.

Yet now it was empty.

King reached over to the phone and called room 1010. No answer.

He called the room where the Johnsons had been staying. No answer.

King stood.

"I know what this must look like to you guys," he said. "But she was here."

"Pillowcase over her head and sock in her mouth?" Mundie asked without humor. "Clean sock or dirty?"

King decided it would be better to let that remark slide. "Our parents were on board with taking her hostage and getting your help. They said they'd wait until I brought you back."

King shook his head, speaking to himself out loud. "How can someone waltz in here and force six adults and two guys my age to leave with them?"

Evans said, "Promise to hurt one of them. The others would go along."

King closed his eyes. Disaster.

He opened them again. "One way to find out."

"If you're not scamming me," Mundie said.

King wanted to make a remark about agents making a living by scamming each other or people around them, but he said nothing. Instead, he pulled out his phone and sent a text to MJ.

At the room. Nobody here. Can't find a note telling me where you went. Even my pajamas are gone.

As if MJ had been waiting, a return text appeared within seconds.

Mack said we were too exposed there. He arranged for a ferry. We're all back on the island. Didn't want to text you in case you were in a delicate situation.

King looked up from the screen at the three agents. "They are definitely in trouble," he said.

He passed the phone to Evans, who read both texts aloud for the benefit of the others.

"That confirms for you that they're in trouble?" Mundie said, not hiding his irritation. "If this goes sideways, I've just put my career on hold for a decade."

"We learned it from Evans," King said. "To use code phrases to confirm our identities. Someone else is using MJ's phone to reply. I used "pajamas" in my text. That would tell MJ it was coming from me. And he should have responded with something like "Mr. Pajamas is in the White House."

"You call the president Pajamas?" This from Mundie with zero trace of a smile.

"MJ did last night," King said. "It was good for a laugh. Things aren't so funny now."

"You got that straight," Mundie said.

Moore said, "You're sure they didn't go to McNeil Island. Positive?"

"If someone else sent that text to try to get us to believe that's where they are, that's exactly where they are not," King said. "But I'm thinking that maybe we should have the rest of this conversation in room 1010."

"You told us that room is bugged," snapped Mundie. Then a small smile returned to his face. "Of course. The room is bugged."

"And," Moore said, "if I understand correctly, nobody gave any hints to Kelli Isaac that they knew it was bugged, right?"

"Right," King said.

King glanced at the clock. It was probably the five hundredth time he'd checked the time.

It wasn't slowing down.

CHAPTER 51

In room 1010, King said to Evans, "I'm online. Here's the USB port."

Evans said to King, "You realize how much trust it takes for us to let you upload those files to your Dropbox account? Delamarre would probably pay you a million dollars for proof like that. So would a newspaper, for proof that the CIA was behind the false charges against him."

Sunlight poured through the windows that gave such a spectacular view of the waterfront. As if it were just another gorgeous day in Seattle. For King, it was the opposite. The countdown for Amanda was moving inexorably forward, and added to that was the almost overwhelming stress of thinking that his parents, his friends, and his friends' parents were probably in the same kind of danger.

King looked down at a piece of paper that had their scripted conversation in place. They'd spent ten minutes in the lobby writing it and then photocopied it so each person had one.

"I don't want a million dollars," King said. "I want my family and friends to be safe."

Mundie said, "All of this on the assumption that they aren't on McNeil Island? Why don't we just go there first?"

"I promise you," King said, "if that had been MJ sending me the text, he would have used the code words to prove it was him. Let me send a text to MJ's phone. If MJ isn't the one holding the phone, we'll find out right away. The files I'm uploading are going to be worth a lot to the person who's really on the other end."

"I'm not sure offering an exchange is a great idea," Moore said on cue. "We won't have any control."

"You want Amanda, I want my friends," King said. "Do we have a choice?"

Mundie said, "How about we just promise Delamarre that the CIA will put out a press release that the terrorism charges were based on faulty intelligence? That was the original plan anyway, once he gave the CIA what we wanted."

Evans glanced at his own paper and kept following along. "I'm with the kid on this one. Let's see if we can get him a meeting with Delamarre and let him do some negotiating for us. We get Amanda and everyone else. He turns over the files to Delamarre. If the CIA doesn't send out the press release, Delamarre can use those files to force it to happen."

"What if Delamarre decides to make those files public anyway?" Mundie said. "This is my career on the line."

"He knows if he keeps antagonizing the CIA," Moore said, "he'll spend the rest of his life wondering if locked doors are good enough to keep him safe. On the other hand, once you give him the files he wants, he'll have no reason to keep Amanda or the others, and no reason to disclose those files to damage the CIA after we issue our press release saying he's innocent of the charges. Life goes back to normal for everyone, including him."

"Guys," King said. They were down to the final lines of the script. After that, everything would depend on the response to the text King would send out. "The upload is complete. And time is ticking. We're decided, right? I can send a text to MJ's phone and offer a deal?"

"With my reluctance," Mundie said, still reading from his paper. "Someone make a note of that. I'm not happy about this, but I say yes, go ahead."

CHAPTER 52

"Nervous?" King asked Evans.

They were in one of the black company SUVs, parked in a no-parking zone in downtown Seattle, where the shadows of skyscrapers formed an artificial canyon. Evans kept checking his cell phone as if that would make things happen faster.

"Can't think of any reason why I should be," Evans said. "You?"

"You mean reasons like my friends and family have disappeared?" King countered, trying to play it cool. "A girl is going to be drowned before tomorrow morning? Your career is on the line?"

"National security is at stake," Evans said. "Don't forget that. And the real prospect that I could be jailed for all the lines I've crossed."

"So," King said, "you're nervous."

"Yup. You?"

"Yup," King said in the same casual tone, thinking that now, if ever, was a time that a panic attack could be expected and justified. So why wasn't it hitting? Too many things to focus on?

"Worst part is waiting," Evans said. "Out on an operation, that's one thing. If you're in an ambush situation, you find a spot, settle in, breathe slow, and let your heart rate slow down. But who knows where this phone call will send us? Or whether we can secure the perimeters?"

"I trust you," King said.

"Thanks," Evans said.

"Which is crazy when you think about it," King said. "It seems to me like national security is built on layers and layers of falsehoods. How many times a week in your job do you have to lie to people?"

Evans snorted. "Well, if we told the truth—"

King spoke slowly, thinking out loud. "That's what I mean. You can't let the bad guys know what you know, and you can't let the good guys know what you know. It's all about secrets and lies."

"Think it can be any different?"

"Don't know," King said. "I wish it could. I wish when the president of the United States makes a public declaration, I could believe it instead of wondering what is really hidden from us and whether it's being done for the good of the people or for the good of the politician. And if we can't trust the president to speak the truth, why should we expect anyone to tell the truth? And once that happens—or maybe it's already at that point—what kind of society is this? Worst thing is, I'm as bad as anyone. I've been lying to my parents for weeks, hiding how I feel about stuff."

"Stuff?"

"I get scared," King said. "Without warning. Without reason."

Evans snorted. "So the good news is that at least right now you have a reason?"

"Yeah," King said, okay with Evans' attempt at making the mood lighter. "Great news."

The phone chirped.

Evans answered and held it to his ear. He listened and nodded. Listened some more.

"Understood," Evans said.

And hung up.

Evans started the engine and put the SUV into gear. He checked his rearview mirror and slipped into the traffic.

"It's a go," Evans said. "Delamarre set up the meet. Do I need to go over anything with you again?"

"Nope," King said. "I know you've got my back."

CHAPTER 53

"I'll bet you're surprised at how few precautions I took to set this up," Ron Delamarre said to King. "Especially given that the CIA is involved with this."

It was a hotel conference room, only blocks away from where King had sent a series of texts from room 1010 about an hour earlier. The blinds were closed and the main lights off with small track lights illuminating Delamarre, who sat behind a table.

To King, Delamarre was instantly recognizable from the newspaper photographs. He was a long-haired, middle-aged guy with blond streaks in his hair. He wore jeans and a pink polo shirt, sleeves rolled up. His right hand held a revolver.

King didn't say it, but he was surprised at how little fear he felt when he saw the weapon. If anything warranted a panic attack, this was it.

"Not really surprised that you feel like you're in a strong position," King said. "You've still got Amanda and my friends and the families as hostages somewhere. That's going to prevent anyone from making a move to take you down. At least that's the way I'd see it if I were you. You don't need a gun in this situation."

"Holding a weapon makes me feel better," Delamarre said. "You wired?"

"Yes," King said. "You'd expect that, right?"

"Of course. There's a reason I chose this conference room. It's got the equipment to let me video this conversation and stream it to the cloud as it happens. If I don't get back to my safe place within two hours and put in a password, the contents of the cloud will go to all the major media outlets across America. It's called a dead man's switch. You familiar with that?"

"Vaguely," King said.

"Doesn't matter if you are," Delamarre said. "Your handlers are, and they're listening to every word, so I probably won't need this revolver. But it's good for them to know I'm holding it."

"Mind pointing it away from me?" King said. "I think better when I'm not nervous."

"No problem," Delamarre said. He tilted the barrel at a spot well to the side of King. "How about you just give me access to the files I need?"

"The same files you wanted when you took Amanda as hostage?"

"Don't get tedious," Delamarre said. "We both know this conversation is recorded. I have no problem admitting I was behind that because once she's released, the CIA is going to want to bury all of this. And I'll bury it with them as long as I'm no longer public enemy number one."

"Can you satisfy my curiosity?" King said. "Tell me what software you developed that makes the CIA want you badly enough to fake the terrorism charges against you."

"Specifically, no. Trust me, you don't want the burden of carrying around classified information. They'll put an invisible tether on you for the rest of your life. But in general, I'll tell you something you may already know. For decades, the CIA has tried to be one step ahead in psywar."

"Sigh war?"

Delamarre showed his first signs of impatience. "Psy—p-s-y."

Then he relaxed and smiled as he waved his hands. "It's a good thing you're making me spell this out. You know, in case I need to activate my dead man's switch and release this conversation to the media."

"Sir," King said, "the revolver is pointing at me again."

"Accident," Delamarre said, tilting it sideways again. "Let's get back to psywar. Psychological warfare. From inflicting mass terror in ancient wars, to using social media and deceptions in modern times. It ranges from using loud sounds to taking over television stations and making false broadcasts. The CIA has done it all and is always looking for more. What I developed is going to be very effective, but it depends on secrecy. If people knew what the CIA has, the weapon would be ruined. I was given the contract, but my company did such a good job with it, I decided it would serve the world better if people put it to commercial use, not psywar use."

Delamarre laughed again. "And it would make me more money. To license it would make me look like a hero. And once I told that to the CIA, they squeezed me with the false terrorism charges."

"You're saying this, aware of how it will sound if the media listens to this conversation, right?"

"Sure," Delamarre said. "It's how you fight back in a psywar. So, how about either give me access to the files you promised or tell me that you're running some kind of bluff."

Delamarre lifted the revolver. "By the way, it's no accident I'm pointing this at you now. I'm going to start a countdown. I want the code by the time I get to zero."

"You want a video of you shooting a kid uploaded to the media?"

"Why not?" Delamarre said. "It's the CIA's fault. Ten. Nine."

"I've got my phone with me," King said. "Tell me what email address I can use to send you the access code."

"Eight. Seven."

"Now you're really making me nervous," King said. He moved sideways a step. The dark hole of the revolver's barrel followed him. He had nowhere to hide, thinking that Mundie's promise had come true again. "You can have the files!"

"Six. Five."

King realized in that moment he was dealing with a crazy person. Maybe the CIA had known that all along.

"Evans!" King said. "Now!"

"Four. Three."

King heard a door crash open behind him.

"Stop!" Evans yelled. "I'm your target! Not the kid."

"You're CIA?" Delamarre asked.

"Yes," Evans said. "We can work something out. I promise."

The revolver stayed on King, and Delamarre continued in a monotone. "Two. One."

Evans began to dive toward Delamarre, but King could see that it would be too late. Delamarre didn't remove his focus or aim from King.

"Zero."

Incredible. King knew he was going to die, and yet he felt an overwhelming peace cover him. *Bang!*

The sound of Delamarre's revolver deafened King.

Two more horrendous explosions. King saw the intense white flare from the revolver barrel each time. Yet he felt no pain.

Is this what dying is like? King wondered. *Time slows down, and the soul perceives things in an entirely new way?* He shouldn't be hearing things and seeing things if he was gone from his body. Should he?

Another horrendous explosion.

King saw Evans dive straight through Delamarre and crash into the wall.

King looked down at his chest. No holes, no blood, no pain.

"Kind of cool, isn't it," Delamarre's image said to King. Evans was getting up, groggy and confused.

"I'm here," Delamarre said, "but I'm not."

Evans staggered to Delamarre and with a sling of his arm, put Delamarre in a head lock. Except when Evans pulled, his arm went through Delamarre's neck. Like Delamarre was a ghost.

"Wish I could stick around and chat," Delamarre said, "but it's time to go."

As Evans clutched again at Delamarre, the man simply disappeared.

CHAPTER 54

Mundie said to Evans and Moore, "We broke every rule in the book, and now we're paying the price."

Moore shook his head. "We didn't have time to pull together a bigger operation. The review board will see it that way. It was a sound plan considering the restraints we faced."

Mundie closed his eyes. "Wrong. There's a Feeb here in Seattle who is going to love to hear that I'm ending my career in Kansas. Our only hope was getting Delamarre, not the handwritten sign in a cabin in the Cascades."

Mundie and Moore had just joined King and Evans in the conference room. The plan had been to use King to distract Delamarre and buy time to use CIA technology to track down the transmissions of the bugs planted in room 1010.

"Sign?" Evans said.

"Yeah." Mundie rubbed his face with both hands. "The lead guy on our chopper team snapped a photo and emailed it to me. You can see for yourself."

Mundie held out his phone, and Evans took it and shared it with King. They saw a whiteboard on an easel with a message written in blue letters.

You should have wondered why I used primitive bugs that even kids could find. And why I made it so easy for you to track the transmissions. But then, I built a billion-dollar software company, and you wear suits and work for the government.

It would have been funny to King, but they were no closer to rescuing Amanda or his friends and family.

Mundie looked at Evans and at the empty conference room. "And obviously Delamarre faked us out on setting up a meeting here too."

"Well," Evans said, "funny thing about that. I'm still not sure I can believe what happened."

"Try me," Mundie said. "How much worse could our day get?"

King's phone buzzed. Incoming FaceTime call. From MJ.

"Got something here," King told the agents. "MJ is calling. Or his phone is calling. I should accept the invite, right?"

"Yes," Mundie said. "Absolutely. Like I said, how much worse can it get?"

CHAPTER 55

King wasn't surprised to see Delamarre's face appear on the screen of his iPhone. The man was wearing a pink polo shirt, just like the digital image of the man who had just shot him and disappeared.

"King," Delamarre said, a warm grin on his face. "Good to see you again. Still checking for bullet holes?"

King's first impulse was to snap an insult, but Delamarre's good humor was infectious, and King found himself liking the guy.

"Nope," King said. "I had to move on and change my diapers."

"Realistic, wasn't it. I felt bad doing it but didn't see any other way."

Mundie tapped King, motioning for the phone. King handed it to Mundie, who gave Delamarre a stone-faced look. "Whatever game you're playing—"

The phone went dark.

Mundie was stunned, and it showed on his face.

The phone buzzed again. Incoming FaceTime invitation from MJ.

King accepted the phone from Mundie and answered. Delamarre's face appeared. "Would you mind telling Mr. Grumpy Pants that he's going to spoil a good party if he keeps going all government official on me? It's pretty easy to hang up halfway through any threat he makes, and then he'll never find out what his too-low clearance level is keeping him from learning about the classified software."

Mundie took the phone from King. "See this smile?"

Mundie smiled at the phone. An obviously fake smile.

"Beautiful," Delamarre said. "And see how much easier it is when people are nice to each other? Can I have the kid back?"

King took the phone back.

"Kinger," Delamarre said, "you can relax. All is good. I don't need any files from you. The video from the conference room should protect me at this point. If I go public with it, the CIA is going to have to admit that the suit who tried jumping my intellitar is one of theirs. And that's going to lead to a whole bunch more stuff that will prove my innocence in the social media world, which is all that matters these days."

"All is good?" King said. "What about a girl that is hours away from drowning?"

"This girl?" Delamarre said. He switched MJ's iPhone from the front camera to the rear camera.

There she was. Amanda. Blonde hair moving in the breeze. Close up, framed just head and shoulders. Wearing a Hawaiian shirt and sipping through a straw from a glass with purple fruit punch and a little umbrella.

"Hey, Kinger," she said. "That's been so sweet of you and your friends to worry about me and help my Paps. It will be great to see you in person—even though I don't believe half of what MJ says about you. Also, can you tell Paps that I feel horrible that he was worried about me? Mom and I came here because she was offered a great job, and part of the condition was that we didn't tell anybody where we were. We had no idea what was happening while we were here."

"Kinger," came MJs voice. His face appeared behind hers. He too was holding a drink with a little umbrella. "You've got to see this place to believe it."

King felt as confused as when he'd believed that Delamarre was firing a revolver at him.

"Who are we working for?" King asked MJ.

MJ answered. "Ron Delamarre. And loving it."

King felt his gut tighten. Wrong answer. Delamarre must have made some kind of threat about the others for Amanda and MJ to pretend everything was okay.

"We used to be working for Mr. Pajamas," MJ said. "But then I learned he was just an intellitar too, so I'm cool for telling a fake president that I would always be ready for briefs that come from him."

Amanda pushed MJ aside. "I saw the whole video. Hilarious."

Now King was even more confused. The code word was there, and Amanda and MJ were bantering as if they were relaxing at a party. But what if Delamarre had forced them to reveal the "Mr. Pajamas" code phrase?

The iPhone switched from rear camera to front camera again, and Delamarre said, "Kinger. Go back to your hotel. I've already got a pilot and my own private chopper waiting on the roof. He'll take you and the suits with you, and we can continue this conversation in person. I've got a couple of lunch baskets on the chopper, but you might want to wait for the buffet I've got set up here. We're poolside. My chef, I will immodestly say, is the best that money can buy."

"No," King said. "Not until I talk to my father."

Delamarre shrugged and turned his face away from the iPhone and shouted. "Mack! You were right. He wants to talk to you."

There was a delay of a few seconds, and then Mack appeared.

"King," Mack said.

"Mack," King said. "I've got a question for you. Answer it right if everything is good."

Mack smiled. "Thanks. I just won my bet with the billionaire big shot."

A twenty-dollar bill appeared in front of Mack's face. Mack was obviously speaking to Delamarre when he said, "That wasn't the deal. You're supposed to donate the money, in person, to a food-bank organization. And it was twenty if I lost to you, and your donation was supposed to be two thousand if you lost to me."

Mack turned back to the iPhone. "Ask. We all want you out here as soon as possible. It's a nice setup. Really nice."

"Blake and the dead man's switch," King said. "What was the last thing you said to me on the cliff the night we escaped?"

Mack grinned. "I hope you will always remember the 'more than life' part, because that's what I asked you to always remember, but technically, the last thing I said was 'go.'"

King would never forget his father's choked words coming at him through the darkness. "*I love you, son. More than life. Always remember that.*"

King grinned back at Mack. "I forgot the 'go,' but technically, you're right. That's all I needed."

Delamarre came back to the screen. "It'll be about fifty-five minutes out here by air. You're good now to catch a ride on the chopper?"

Without hesitation, King answered with one word. "Yes."

"Ta-ta," Delamarre said, wiggling his fingers goodbye. The screen went dark again.

Mundie said to King, "This could still be a trap. You're going to trust Delamarre?"

"No," King said. "I'm going to trust my dad."

CHAPTER 56

On the helicopter, King had tried to stay involved in the conversation of the three CIA agents. They all had headsets, and as promised, lunch baskets were provided.

The inside of the chopper wasn't Spartan, like the ones used by the CIA, but plush with padded leather seats and a minibar and even framed prints on the walls as if it were a tour bus.

But as the chopper headed north and west from Seattle over Puget Sound, King's exhaustion caught up to him. The relief of knowing that his friends and families were safe had drained him completely, and he fell asleep, too tired to even struggle to stay awake as Mundie speculated about intellitars. Weren't they going to find out soon anyway?

King didn't wake until he felt a tapping on his shoulders.

Evans waited until he saw that King was awake.

"Hey, Sleeping Beauty," Evans said to King through the headphones. "We just crossed over Friday Harbor on San Juan Island. We've been tracking our route on a maps app on the iPhone. Check out this estate."

Evans pointed out the window. They might have been five hundred feet high, and the chopper was slowly settling.

To the west, vivid in bright sunshine, was ocean water and other islands on the horizon. Below was a cluster of buildings surrounded by high stone walls that made it look like a small kingdom. In the center was a large swimming pool with turquoise water. A group of people were staring upward at the chopper and waving.

"Cool," King said. He looked at Evans and Moore and Mundie in their suits. "A bit overdressed for a pool party, aren't you?"

*

Delamarre refused to talk business until everyone had eaten lunch. And until Evans and Moore and Mundie had accepted and changed into the shorts and shirts and sandals that Delamarre kept in the pool house as spares for guests.

Now King sat with those four beneath sun umbrellas, overlooking the pool. The five of them. All the others were enjoying pool activities—Amanda and Blake and MJ, along with the parents.

"Let's get this over with," Delamarre said. "I'm in a good mood, and I want to enjoy the sunshine. Then I need to get back to work. Once you clear me, my shares are going to skyrocket. I need to talk to my stockbroker and pick up some big chunks of low-priced stock."

"Don't be so sure," Mundie said.

Delamarre grinned his disarming grin. "Even in shorts and sandals, you still can't get away from that suit, can you."

"My job—"

Delamarre interrupted Mundie. "Your job means doing what is right for America. Mine too. So hear me out, okay?"

"I'm good with that," Moore said. "And I'm the one who should be the maddest. Delamarre was the one who squeezed me by faking a kidnapping of my granddaughter."

Mundie seemed to relax. "Okay. It's a nice day at the pool. I'll listen like a guy wearing shorts and sandals. For now."

"And golf after," Delamarre said. "Great course, just down the road. I'll bet you play to a low handicap, right? Actually, it would be an unfair bet. I did some intel work on you. Your index is 2.3. Got a soft high draw?"

"Doubt I'll have time for golf. I'll need to put together a report and then get ready to resign for messing up."

"In that case," Delamarre said, "why not play golf first? You can't get in any more trouble than what you're facing now."

Oddly, that really seemed to settle Mundie, whose smile this time was genuine. "Tell us about intellitars."

Delamarre's face seemed to go blank for a moment, and then he leaned forward. "How about we make a deal that might save your job? Now that I've got the video I need to protect myself, you go back and tell them you found a way to force me to give you the computer code and sign a deal that delays me going public with the intellitar software for general industry."

Mundie sighed. "Just when I was thinking about golf, you go all suit on me. Look, it's a bad deal for the CIA. I can't go back to anyone with it."

"Sooner or later the technology is going to bust loose," Delamarre said. "You'll only be able to use it a few times until rumors become facts and everyone knows about it anyway. If I give you the code, you'll at least have that window to do as much as you can with it."

"Two years," Mundie said.

"Huh?" Delamarre said.

"Two years before you go public."

"Eighteen months," Delamarre said. "I'm the one in control now. Take it or leave it. Plus I'll cover scholarships for all these kids if they sign a confidentiality agreement for that eighteen-month period."

"Taken," Mundie said.

"And," Delamarre said, "I'll find a way to spin it so it looked like you guys trapped me, and I'll back you up on all accounts."

"Golf course is sounding better and better," Mundie said. "So tell us about intellitars."

CHAPTER 57

Delamarre faced his small audience in one of his two home-theater rooms. This one had a dozen seats. The big one had sixty.

"This is where I first gave life to my own intellitar," he said. "And this is where I set up the FaceTime conversation between Amanda's intellitar and Mr. Moore to convince him she was in danger."

"I didn't know," Amanda was quick to say. "Really."

"She didn't," Delamarre confirmed. "I was able to get the information I needed for the intellitar without her knowledge. That's one of the reasons my software is so incredible. All I really needed was for her to be gone a while so the danger seemed real to Moore. After that, it was a simple matter of tapping into Moore's phone to hear his conversations with Evans and all their plans to try to find her, including the location of the hotel room, and intercepting the email he tried sending to his lawyer. I am, after all, the T. rex of software."

King was fascinated, not necessarily by Delamarre, but by the digital 3-D clone speaking to them. King had a difficult time believing it was not actually Delamarre. And yet the real Delamarre sat beside him, enjoying his own show and watching the intellitar Delamarre.

"Years ago, it began with special effects in movies," the Delamarre intellitar said. "At first it was clumsy, but when technology and software improved, much of the acting was done in front of a blue screen, and the background was put into place behind it. That, of course, is old technology."

Delamarre's intellitar patted his face, and the soft slap of his palm against his cheek was audible in the quietness of the room.

"As you can see," the intellitar said, "it looks real. And sounds real. Unless you walked up here and pushed your hand through me, you'd never know."

"Sir?" came MJ's voice.

"Let me guess," the intellitar said. "You want to try it?"

"Um, yes."

MJ was such a child. King loved him for it.

"Go ahead."

MJ got up from his seat. He walked toward the intellitar. Then through it.

"Cool," MJ said.

"It is cool," the real Delamarre said beside King. "Very cool. Worth hundreds of millions in the real world once the CIA gets through with it."

MJ whirled on the intellitar. "Fist bump?"

"He's going to do the idiotic starburst," King whispered to Delamarre. "He does that all the time."

Sure enough. MJ finished the fist bump with wiggly fingers. Looking satisfied, he took his seat in the theater with everyone else.

"So here's what goes into creating an intellitar," the fake Delamarre said. "Voice recordings. As much information as possible about the person. A complete video scan from all angles. Unfortunately, at this point, we are limited to an intellitar that is clothed the way the real person was clothed."

Evans spoke in King's direction to the real Delamarre. "But the intellitar is reacting up there without any direction from you. How's that possible?"

"Let me take that question," the intellitar said. "Think of iPhone's Siri, and then ramp that up three more generations. AI is at the point where —"

"AI?" Mrs. Johnson said. She was sitting at the back. Probably knitting.

"Artificial intelligence," the intellitar said. "Computers are now at the point where a human can have a typed conversation on a screen without knowing whether the response is coming from another human or from a computer. Our software is similar to how Siri handles it. A giant mainframe computer, responding through the cloud. It stores information about the intellitar, it has access to everything on Google, and it uses the voice of the person set up as the intellitar."

"How mobile is it?" Moore said.

"We're at the first generation of this," the intellitar said. "Not very mobile at all. To make the sound seem as if it's coming from my mouth, directional speakers are triangulating the sound at about where my face is. We also need dozens of small microphones in the room to catch any conversations. And of course, we need the dozens of projectors lining this room to send light rays to come in at 360 degrees to give this digital clone the three-dimensional effect."

King spoke. He found himself directing the question to the intellitar instead of the real Delamarre beside him—that's how mesmerizing all of this was. "There weren't any projectors in the room where I was speaking to you in downtown Seattle. And I don't see any here either."

"That's because each projector's lens opening is about the size of a dime, and I've built them into these walls. And I knew you were going to be curious about the conference room in Seattle. That's an easy answer. After I set up the prototype here, I leased that conference room permanently and did the same there. I needed a place to demonstrate the intellitar. Somewhere close to my own software company location. I could have asked you to show up immediately, but I waited so it looked like the real Delamarre needed time to fly in and meet with you."

"So at this point," Moore said, "the use will be limited to those who can set up a place dedicated to the intellitar."

"Yes," came the answer. "At a cost of three hundred million per prototype. Easily affordable to governments. Or businesses that can afford to purchase a personal jumbo jet."

The intellitar became more animated, like a salesman. "With the next-generation prototype and something that is portable, government figures can address the public without fear of being assassinated."

Blake said, "And you could make it look like one of the terrorist leaders in the Middle East is telling all his followers to put down their guns."

"Yes." This voice came from the real Delamarre, who stood and walked to the front and faced them with his intellitar. They were identical twins, differing only in the clothes they wore. "But it won't fool people for long, and that's when its value to governments as a weapon or a defense will be diminished. I want this to be available for the world to use. It can help people in so many different ways. Real-life hologram meetings—stuff like that."

"And help the value of your stocks," Moore said.

Both the intellitar and the real Delamarre grinned.

"Of course."

Both bowed.

When the real Delamarre stood, he clicked a remote hidden in his hand, and the intellitar faded away.

CHAPTER 58

King sat in a poolside lounge chair. Wrapped in a luxury robe, he held a drink with a little umbrella in it. As he watched the bottom edge of the sun creep down to the ocean's horizon, he reflected on what he'd learned earlier.

Intellitars.

What Delamarre had been able to accomplish through compartmentalized research divisions was in essence a form of digital cloning with new hardware and new software.

King suspected this was just the beginning.

And King also believed Delamarre was right about another thing. Soon enough, the technology would leak out no matter how hard the CIA fought it, and the CIA would lose the effectiveness of it. In the public world, people would find plenty of applications for intellitars.

And, King thought sadly, plenty of misuses for it.

He was getting sleepy again. He knew why—he was finally at the end of the roller-coaster ride of the past few days. And he hadn't felt any panic attacks during the afternoon.

He didn't feel the need to be near his parents. It might have been because he knew they were safe. Or maybe because he knew he could handle the stress.

King thought, however, it was more than that. In the final numbers of the countdown of Delamarre's intellitar, King had fully believed he would die. When the digital revolver was fired, he'd accepted that his life was over. And he'd been granted a peace he didn't expect. It was like a certainty that leaving his body was the beginning of a journey he didn't need to fear. A warmth still filled him and drove away any sense of dread. The warmth would fade, he expected, but he'd still be able to remind himself of it, just as he could always remind himself of his father's last words on the cliff.

As King began to drift away into his sleep, he smiled at one thing Delamarre had told him privately after the meeting with Moore and Evans and Mundie.

Delamarre had already developed a type of laser beam that was harmless to people but would cut through intellitars to expose them as digital clones. Of course, Delamarre had said, he was going to wait six months or so before he offered it to the CIA.

That might have been his final thought before falling asleep, except Mack strolled up to the chairs.

"Mind if I join you?" Mack asked.

"Was hoping you would," King answered.

Both watched the sunset in friendly silence. As the final piece of the sun dipped below the horizon, Mack let out a sigh of contentment.

"Glad everything is good," Mack said.

"Me too," King answered.

"How good?" Mack asked. "And I'm not looking for an answer where you try to hide from me your phobia of leaving the island."

King straightened in surprise.

Mack answered the question before King could voice it. "King. We're your parents. It's our job to know stuff about you that you think we don't know."

"And hide from me that you know it?"

Mack refused to get drawn into an argument, and deflected the question with a laugh. "Like you were hiding it from us? Our physician told us it was probably panic attacks, based on what we could report to him about you. Was that your conclusion?"

King slumped back. Then a thought hit him.

"Hey," he said. "That's why you worked so hard to get me off the island with MJ and Blake."

"Didn't know what else to do. Wasn't going to leave you in the nest forever."

"Huh," King said. "It's kind of like you betrayed me, making me get on a helicopter."

"Harsh," Mack said. "I'd rather you didn't think of it that way. From our perspective, Ella and I wished you would have opened up about what was bothering you."

"Didn't want you worried," King said. "It was already bad enough, getting through the time that she was in a coma. You mad?"

"Son," Mack said, "in a perfect world, none of us would have to wear masks. But there's a part of being human that makes it irresistible to spend so much time pretending to be something we are not. I'm as guilty of it as the next person, and there are days it feels like old crusty skin. When you love someone, and you are loved back, that's the best chance we have of being who we are, and even then, we have to fight wearing a mask. The situation makes me sad, but no, I'm not mad at you. Let's both try to build on that and do better in the future. You good with that?"

"Yup," King said, feeling drowsy again.

But sleep was not to be his. Mack patted him on the knee. "Your friends are on the way, so I'm out of here. Last thing I need is MJ to ask me another question, like have I ever wondered about a world with no hypothetical situations."

Mack bolted. If MJ wasn't telling knock-knock jokes, he had his list of weird questions, like why 7-Eleven stores had locks on the doors if they were always open.

MJ and Blake plunked themselves on chairs beside him.

"Kinger," MJ said. "You grooving it out here?"

"Grooving it," King said.

"Hey," MJ said. "I was wondering. If nothing sticks to Teflon, what makes Teflon stick to the pan?"

"And I was wondering something too," King said. He'd prepared for this a few days earlier. "Why is it a shipment when you move something by car, but when a ship moves it, it's called cargo?"

As MJ struggled to answer that one, King finally fell asleep.

END NOTES

Lying

Humans do tell lies, and according to one researcher, this "may be an unavoidable part of human nature."

Deceit as a part of human nature and its impact on our public and private lives—these topics are well worth discussing. For example, when politicians and spies lie for the good of their country, are they eroding the public trust?

To start exploring the damage lies can do, check out the thought-provoking book *Lying: Moral Choice in Public and Private Life* by Sissela Bok. Be warned, however—it might force you to examine the lies you tell in your own life!

The BBC has provided a series of brief and helpful articles about lying.[1] Use them to start a discussion with your friends and family about the ethics of lying.

Psywar

Since prehistoric times, psychological warfare (pyswar) has been a part of battle tactics, but not always to induce terror. For example, Alexander the Great held on to his conquered territories by inducing the local elites to join Greek administration and culture. Similarly, Roman emperors offered citizenship to conquered tribes.

More often, however, pyswar is used to frighten opponents into submission and to defeat the will of the enemy. In the thirteenth century, Genghis Khan showed mastery of this by having each of his soldiers carry three torches at night to give the illusion of a much larger army. During the daytime, his army tied objects to the tails of horses to raise larger clouds of dusts and give the same impression.

---

[1] www.bbc.co.uk/ethics/lying/lying_1.shtml.

Modern pyswar began in World War One with propaganda delivered by flyers dropped from airplanes. More recently, the CIA has broadcast propaganda on pirated television channels.

It should be noted that pyswar is often based on deceit.

Intellitars

Intelligent avatars are on our technological horizon. Consider these related current technologies and trends:

Lifenaut. The website www.lifenaut.com "offers participation in a long-term computer science research project that explores how technology may one day extend life through digital technology." Lifenaut allows you to upload your photos, videos, and documents to a digital archive and create a computer-based avatar.

Artificial intelligence. AI continues to advance. World-renowned scientist Stephen Hawking warns that "the development of full artificial intelligence could spell the end of the human race." After all, nearly twenty years ago, Deep Blue, a chess-playing computer developed by IBM, defeated a world-champion chess master. Deep Blue was capable of evaluating 200 million positions per second.

The Turing Test, named after computer pioneer Alan Turing, examines whether a machine can show intelligent behavior that cannot be distinguished from human intelligence. "A human judge engages in natural language conversations with a human and a machine designed to generate performance indistinguishable from that of a human being. All participants are separated from one another. If the judge cannot reliably tell the machine from the human, the machine is said to have passed the test. The test does not check the ability to give the correct answer to questions; it checks how closely the answer resembles typical human answers. The conversation is limited to a text-only channel, such as a computer keyboard and screen, so that the result is not dependent on the machine's ability to render words into audio."[2]

A Turing Test competition at England's prestigious University of Reading was organized in June of 2014 to mark the sixtieth anniversary

---

[2] "Turning Test," en.wikipedia.org/wiki/Turing_test.

of Alan Turing's death. It also marked what many consider to be the first time that AI passed the test—a chatter bot convinced 33 percent of contest judges that it was human.

And of course, digital voice assistants, such as Apple's Siri, Microsoft's Cortana, and Google Now, are part of many people's everyday lives.

Digital cloning. The final technology necessary to make intellitars a reality—digital cloning—is continuing to advance. In 2008, Digital Emily introduced many people to "image metrics" on a YouTube video.[3] Most viewers were surprised to discover that her face was completely computer generated.

In 2012, the University of Southern California began the Digital Ira project to "create a real-time, photoreal digital human character which could be seen from any viewpoint, any lighting, and could perform realistically from video performance capture even in a tight closeup."[4] You can see the results for yourself on YouTube.[5]

Holograms. Can a digital clone really be converted into a three-dimensional hologram? Stephen D. Smith of the University of Southern California demonstrates that a conversation with a hologram is now eerily realistic.[6] He shows how holographic technology is being used to allow Holocaust survivors to interact with students and to keep survivors' stories alive after the survivors are gone. If you prefer reading instead of watching, see "Is Digital Cloning the Future of Movie Making?" on the CBS News website.[7] Note that the lab for this digital cloning project "gets much of its funding from the Department of Defense."

Human consciousness. Lifenaut, the website that is dedicated to eternalizing humans through digital cloning, is based on this: "By combining detailed data about a person future, AI software will be able to reanimate the person's consciousness." It uses a Mindfile, which is "a database containing a person's unique and essential characteristics,

---

[3] www.youtube.com/watch?v=UYgLFt5wfP4

[4] ict.usc.edu/prototypes/digital-ira/

[5] www.youtube.com/watch?v=RzKb6YVAyQI. The digital face speaks at about the sixty-second mark.

[6] www.youtube.com/watch?v=IAk9WODP43Q. See especially at 2:45! If you prefer reading, see

[7] www.cbsnews.com/news/future-of-movies-digital-cloning-in-maleficent/

made up of memories, photos, videos, documents, conversation logs, and personality test results." In short, this project goal is to graft human consciousness into a clone for a version of immortality. [8]

The CIA

As for the CIA developing and using intellitars for pyswar, some would declare this to be nothing but fiction.

[8] www.cbsnews.com/news/future-of-movies-digital-cloning-in-maleficent/

Also from Sigmund Brouwer and Harvest House Publishers

Dead Man's Switch

William King's mind is reeling because of the email he received, partly because of the secrets it claims to unveil and partly because it was sent from his friend Blake—who drowned two weeks earlier trying to escape the island.

Worse, the email threatens that King's father is involved in criminal activity on McNeil Island, where King's dad works at a high-security prison. King embarks on a high-tech and high-stakes search to hunt down answers he's afraid to learn. But when King becomes the hunted, he has to decide—whom can he trust?

If you love a great mystery and the quest for justice, you'll think about this book long after you read the last chapter.